Crashin' the Real

One woman's search for truth, justice . . .

and Steven Tyler

by

Deb Hoag

Crashin' the Real

Published by Dog Horn Publishing, 2009.

Copyright © Deb Hoag 2009

Cover Art © Matt Truiano (front), Richard Ware (back)

Publisher: Adam Lowe

Line-Editor/Developer: Victoria Hooper

Dog Horn Publishing

United Kingdom

www.doghornpublishing.com

A CIP catalogue record for this book is available from the British Library.

First edition printed and bound in the UK.

Dedication: This book is dedicated to my stunningly wonderful husband, Chuck, also known as The Handsomest Man in the World; and to the kids – his, mine and ours – none of whom are allowed to read this until they're thirty.

Acknowledgements: This book is only possible due to the support, friendship and constant encouragement from my awesome friend, editor and publisher, Adam Lowe of *Polluto* and Dog Horn Publishing. May you have every good thing, darling, in abundance. To Miki Dark, who took precious time from his plot to overthrow the universe in order to give me support and encouragement in the wee hours. To Victoria Hooper, who *got* everything, amazingly enough; no one could be kinder (or firmer!). To Bill Highsmith, the king of the emergency, last-minute readers, to Richard Ware, the best tattoo artist on the eastern seaboard and illustrator extraordinaire, and all my other good friends at *Polluto* and at Hatrack River, for endless reading, thoughtful comments and a good boot up the ass once in a while – thanks!

No llamas were harmed in the making of this book. Any resemblance to anyone, real, fictional or imagined, is solely the product of the author's lurid imagination, and has no basis in reality whatsoever.

Now

Chapter One: Sucks to be Me

First band I ever saw live, I was seventeen; the band was Aerosmith. Tyler a Demented Juicy Monkey Sex God, in a striped spandex jumpsuit. Joe Perry all blistering heat in intimate rock-n-roll incest next to him. Didn't know if Perry wanted to fuck him, or kill him, while visions of hash oil danced in my head. I loved him. I loved them all. Something clicked inside my head and everything was okay.

★

Twenty years later, I was writing a column, "All About Eve", for *Whipt! Detroit's Alternative Entertainment Magazine*. *Whipt!* wasn't just some boring entertainment mag, though. It was a jittery explosion of art, parties, bands and politics chaotically crammed between a folded full-color cover. *Whipt! was* actually published in the city, in a grimy hundred-year-old building with chipped marble floors and gilt-trimmed ceilings. A lot of publications claiming Detroit-hood were actually based in the suburbs, and the writers involved had no more idea of what it meant to be a Detroiter than a gladiola knows what it means to be a spice cake.

I walked into work and looked around the editorial department. It was a big, open space, with half-walls separating the cubicles by the big windows. You could tell in one quick sweep who was there and who was MIA.

Framed posters made from past *Whipt!* covers decorated the brick walls. My favorite just happened to be a full-length shot of me, laying on the editorial department conference table in a seductive pose, a cigarette

4

smoldering in the ashtray in front of me, a tumbler of Jack right next to it, and a bright green apple in my left hand. The headline read: *Get a Taste of Eve.*

I crossed over to Loyola, the new receptionist, whom I had known for years and thoroughly loathed, and gave her the usual greeting. "Tyler call this morning?"

She rolled her beady little eyes, like she had somehow become confused over the fact that a star columnist trumped a puny receptionist. "First of all, it hasn't been morning for hours. Secondly, no, *Evangeline*, Steven Tyler did not and never will call you. Just like he didn't call yesterday, and he didn't call the day before that, and he didn't call the day before that. And like he won't call tomorrow, or the next day, or the next."

She knew my full name. In order to know that, she had to have been snooping in my personnel file. "Loyola, you're such a bitch." I started to walk away. I'm mature.

"At least *I* wasn't born with my eyeliner already tattooed on." There was a snotty little sniff that punctuated that remark, one of those sarcastic, snarky sniffs.

So, I did what any mature woman would do. I picked up a letter off her desk, took out my lighter, and lit it on fire. Then I threw the burning letter back on her desk. I had the satisfaction of seeing that snarky look disappear into a grimace of horror as she watched the papers on her desk go up in flames.

I gave her a sympathetic look. "Oh, Loyola, whatever are you going to do? Here, let me help." I reached out and pulled the fuck-me roses from the vase on her desk.

5

"Here, hold these for a minute."

Passing the flowers to Loyola, I helpfully dumped the vase of water on the desk.

The fire was out, but water was spreading everywhere. Her keyboard was making funny sizzling noises. Loyola sat there for a minute, blinking like a moron. Then a flood of cold water hit her lap. She jumped up, cursing and frantically trying to brush water and ash off her fancy dress.

My work *here* was done. I turned and walked away, not wanting to gloat in her defeat. Kindness is a quality of great leaders.

Behind me, Loyola called in a thick voice, "You're just an old, black-leather bitch. You look like Joan Jett's mother. Wait till I tell Peter!"

Joan Jett's *mother*? Who was she kidding? And who the hell was Peter? Current boyfriend? Big brother? No problem. I have a Glock in my purse for emergencies. Satisfied, I went to my office.

★

"I heard you set the receptionist on fire." Blue, the publisher, had called an editorial/management team meeting, which usually only happened when somebody really pissed off an advertiser.

"No, I set the desk on fire. I haven't lit a receptionist since the nineties."

He raised an eyebrow at me.

"Things are changing, Eve. You can't go around setting people's desks on fire and expect them to take it just because they answer phones and you write a column."

I looked at him, stumped. "Why not?"

"Maybe *I* can explain that to you, Ms. Petra," said a man at the far end of the table. I had never seen him before, but we had a lot of folks float in and out of editorial meetings – the pissed off advertiser, for example, people hustling a product Blue was interested in, new employees, blah, blah, blah.

The old guy dragged his saggy ass out of the chair and rose to his feet, placing his hands flat on the table in front of him, so that he could peer down at me authoritatively.

"Explain away," I said, going for breezy. Who the hell was this jerk?

"Well, Ms. Petra," he said ponderously, "Even those who consider themselves above all us working stiffs have rules that we have to follow. That includes not terrorizing, threatening and intimidating, or otherwise opening *Whipt!* to legal action for providing an unsafe working environment."

I tipped my chair back and put my booted feet on the table. "Who's gonna sue us?"

The man's face grew red, his eyes bulged, and he hollered out the answer. "Everyone, if you don't learn to conduct yourself appropriately, you overpaid, talentless hack!"

It was amazing. Little drops of spittle were flying through the air. When he finished shouting, he stood straight and took off his glasses to wipe them with a care that was diagnosable.

"She's not talentless, and she's not a hack. Little crazy, maybe, but you don't have to listen to what she says, just read what she writes." I gave Blue a dirty look, and he shrugged a *what did you want me to say?* gesture at me.

I leaned over to Blue. "Who the hell is this guy?" I whispered. I was afraid if I said anything else and he heard it, he could go right into cardiac arrest.

7

Blue leaned toward me to whisper in my ear, "He's the new owner, and he's Loyola's uncle. I just sold *Whipt!* to him."

*

Peter Beater was a successful entrepreneur, who thought the sun shone out the Pope's ass. He was not only Loyola's uncle, but when his half-brother died in Vietnam, he moved right in and married Mia Monk, Loyola's mom – she became Mia Monk-Beater.

Beater himself was best known for taking Detroit's last great album rock station, WBAX, and turning it into a 24-hour advertising broadcast, occasionally interrupted by insipid pop tunes. When he sold it, he made millions. Now, he was the owner of *Whipt!* and the only person in the place who *wasn't* terrified was Loyola, who had been promoted immediately to publisher's assistant.

Beater didn't fire me outright, the devious putz. Instead, he said the two words guaranteed to strike fear in the heart of anyone who has devoted their lives to rock-and-roll, life underground, or the democratic party: drug test.

Twenty-four hours later, going through every proper channel, and with Loyola grinning at me like a hyena from behind his back, Peter Beater notified me that I was fired. And, because my drug test confirmed I had violated company policy by way of using illegal substances, I wasn't going to get severance pay or unemployment, either. What the hell did I care? I'd have a new job before the end of the day, and I was ready to take on a new cause: dedicating the rest of my life to humiliating the shit out of Mr. Peter Beater. And with the great new job that was out there waiting for me, I could do it. One column at a time.

*

A week later, I was sure Peter the Beater had sabotaged my career. Everywhere I applied for a column gig, I got turned down. Sometimes with laughter. I called Blue, and he listened to me sympathetically, but wasn't very optimistic. "Face it, Eve, you and I are dinosaurs. Nobody wants a female Hunter Thompson in the editorial department, just like no one wants an old rock dog at the helm. Peter's not a bad guy. He can take *Whipt!* into the future. I not only can't, I don't want to."

He didn't sound very upset about it.

"So what are you going to do, now, Blue?"

I could practically hear him shrugging over the phone. "Take the money and run, babe. Figured I'd go lay around on the beach for a while, then look into something fun. I know a syndication service going cheap. Want me to keep in touch?"

I muttered something vaguely affirmative – Blue and I had known each other for years now, sometimes better than others, and I couldn't quite picture not seeing him on a near daily basis. But there was nothing else I had to say to him at the moment, so we said our goodbyes and I hung up the phone.

Nobody wanted a female Hunter Thompson in their editorial department anymore? I wouldn't have believed it, if I hadn't been around to half-a-dozen magazines already this week, and seen the starched and stuck-up yuppies that were crawling around the places like roaches. Every lobby had ferns. And they had these ridiculous signs up everywhere, "No Smoking," "No Shoes, No Shirt, No Entry". Christ! How could they keep any writers with rules like that?

9

After the phone call with Blue, I admitted defeat and slunk back to my room to lick my wounds. I'd been licking for a while now, and it hadn't helped much. I hadn't realized how much time had gone by, until I woke up one night and heard Grandma Rose outside my bedroom door with Max, trying to convince me to unlock the door.

As they pounded, I clutched a fifth of Jack Black to my chest and pulled a pillow over my head.

"Eve? Evangeline Petra, you have not gotten out of that bed except to go to the bathroom and the liquor store for three days. If you don't come out, right *now*, I'm going to tell Max to bust that damn door down. You hear me, Evangeline?"

I couldn't help it. I cracked up. The idea of Max doing anything more laborious than picking up a paintbrush was more than I could resist. I could hear Max on the other side of the door, making weird muffled noises. He was laughing, too, and trying not to hurt Grandma Rose's feelings by ruining her bluff.

Still, the sound of Max's laughter sounded pretty damn good right now. Laughing sounded pretty damn good right now. I don't think I had laughed one time since the evil words "piss test" were tossed in my face.

I pulled the pillow off my head, and I could hear Max and Grandma Rose having a heated conversation, in whispers, on the other side of my door. I pulled myself into a sitting position and the springs on my bed gave a loud squeak.

"Eve?" called Grandma Rose, "You okay in there?"

"I'm coming *out*," I called back crankily, "That *is* what you wanted, isn't it?" I looked for my slippers. Of course, they couldn't just be where I left

10

them. I had to crawl under the bed for one and wanged my head on the bed frame crawling back out.

"Fuck," I said, clapping a hand to the back of my head.

"Eve, I'm not waiting any longer. Get your ass out here right now, or by God, I'm gonna take a chair and knock that door down myself."

"Jesus, Rosie, don't get your panties in a bunch, I'm coming." I shuffled over to the door, fifth in one hand and head in the other, and had a moment of confusion when I realized I didn't have a hand available to unlock or open the door. Then I jammed the fifth under the elbow of the hand cupping my bruised head, and bobbled the door open.

Light flooded my room, and I blinked my eyes, temporarily blinded.

"Christ, honey, what have you been doing to yourself in there? Taking ugly pills?" That was Max, looking at my streaked mascara and tangled hair.

To the surprise of all three of us, I burst into tears and then took an embarrassingly feeble swing at him. After that, just to make my patheticness completely obvious, I slumped back against the wall and slid down to the floor, and let the tears keep coming.

"Oh, my God, she's totally lost it," said Max in horror. Grandma Rose was just gawking. She'd never seen me take a swing at someone and not connect – hard.

Max sat down on the floor and wrapped his arms around me. I turned my face and rained tears on his sweater. I must have looked worse than even I thought, because he let me.

When I calmed down, I raised my face and blurted out just one of the many things I had become aware of since locking myself in my room.

11

Reality is a *bitter* pill. "Did you know they don't actually have music on MTV anymore?"

He nodded. "I know. We had a funeral for them a few years ago."

Huh.

He turned his face up to Grandma Rose and gave her one of those charming smiles that makes him beloved by old ladies and poodles everywhere. "Miss Rosie, do you have any Valium around? And how about a nice pot of coffee?"

Grandma Rose beamed. "I just got a new prescription. Let me go get 'em, and then I'll start a pot of coffee. You think a doobie would help?"

"Grandma!" I said, shocked.

"Oh, it's not mine. I'm holding it for Frank at the senior center. He thought the nurses were going to search him. But this is a good cause. I'm sure he won't mind."

Off she went, and I sniffed up a bunch of snot, wiped my nose surreptitiously on Max's sweater, and sat back so I could run my fingers under my eyes and blot up tears and melted eye makeup.

I looked at Max, and he looked at me, and we both burst out laughing. I could hear Grandma Rose digging through stuff in her bedroom. Whiskey, dope, Valium and coffee – late-night snack of champions.

To my total amazement, I burst into tears again.

Max looked at me. "You know what you need?"

"What?"

"A hot shower. Come on."

He hauled me to my feet, dragged me into the bathroom, and sat me on the toilet while he got the water going. Then he took away the bottle of

Jack and whipped my shirt off over my head. When I opened my mouth to protest, he stuffed me in the shower.

The hot water burned and stung but it also blasted away several days worth of sweat and old makeup, making me feel nearly human again. I washed my hair and my armpits, then shut the water off. Max handed me a towel, and when I was safely wrapped, pushed me back down onto the toilet seat so that he could brush the tangles out of my hair and run a warm blow dryer over the whole mess.

He was about halfway done when Grandma Rose poked her head back in. "Oh, my, she looks better already! Eve, here's your coffee, two Valium and the joint. I rolled it myself." As I watched, she lifted an unexpectedly tight doobie to her lips and lit it.

I washed down the Valium with hot coffee, then reached for the joint. "Grandma Rose, are you sure you're not helping good ole Frank smoke some of that weed? You're a pretty good roller for a marijuana virgin."

She giggled before she handed the joint to me. "Have to keep up with the kids, Eve. Otherwise you just get old and dried out."

I passed to Max, who gave my hair a final fluff and then shut off the blow-dryer. He took a hit, passed it back to Grandma Rose with a grin, and then tugged on my hand. "Come on, Evie. Let's get you dressed in some clean clothes."

In a few minutes, we were in the dining room, a pot of coffee between us, and shot glasses all around.

We spent most of the night talking. Max went down and fetched my tape case out of the car, and we turned Grandma Rose on to Aerosmith while we decimated Frank's pot stash. Talking, not talking, listening to all my

13

favorite tunes. Grandma Rose laughed her ass off at "Big Ten Inch"; I laughed my ass off watching her. We fired up another doob and Max and I taught her the words. Fragrant rite of passage two decades ago, smokin' a doob with the family. Max and Rose were my family. Grandma Rose was my mom's mom and took me in when mommy dearest dumped me.

The last two decades had been big for Grandma Rose. She had lost her bra, watched Grandpa Joe die, found her identity, and gave up shaving her armpits in favor of finding her G-spot. I remember that last bit. We were having breakfast conversations about G-spots when other kids were still trying to decide whether they wanted cinnamon toast or cereal.

She eventually remarried, to a business type who lived in Grosse Pointe and could follow simple instructions related to her G-spot, and we moved out to the Pointe.

Husband number two kicked off a few years later, and left Grandma the house in Grosse Pointe and a hefty chunk of cash in the bank. Which left Grandma with nothing better to do at midnight on a Tuesday than sitting around shooting the shit with me and Max.

Hours later, Max and I were still sitting at the dining-room table, which was a little the worse for wear. Grandma Rose had conked out a while earlier, and we had step-walked her to bed and tucked her in.

Suddenly restless, I turned to Max. "Let's order some pizza and channel surf – you wanna?"

He nodded and we went back to my bedroom, slouching around companionably on the bed while we argued about satellite channels and waited for pizza. When he put on some lame-ass talk show, I fell back on the bed. On the ceiling above me was my favorite Steven Tyler poster, a still from

14

a performance of "Train Kept a Rollin'".

Cocaine jism eyes in a fallen angel face looked down at me. Mouth carved wide to let the screams come out. Somewhere in his eyes, I thought, there were answers. He looked naked, exposed, pain showing through his skin like bones – but with a glint of Sphinx in his eyes.

Is there a better God to have than rock-n-roll? If there is, I haven't found it yet. Sometimes, I think it's going to break me open and spill me out, jittering guts making electric sparks as they arc free. Instead, it puts me back together.

Some people want to engulf it; some people want to be engulfed. There are women who worship God by shaking their tits at him, or trying to fuck the sacred pole. Men try to ring the Chord from mortal fingers. Not me. I didn't want to play it, write it, fuck it or smoke it. I just wanted to feel it. Feel it beating my heart, ringing my ears, dancing my feet. Being the tuning fork. Maybe that *is* being engulfed. But it's not just notes and words. It's sacredly profane, overwhelming, irresistible.

I wondered if I asked my own personal rock-n-roll God, could he tell me what had happened? What the hell had changed in the world that I had once been on top of? What was I supposed to fucking do about it? Some people ask God. I ask Steven Tyler.

The pizza came, and we stuffed ourselves, then lay around some more, TV turned low. Max painted my nails for me. I had almost nodded off, when my eyes snapped open and I stared right into Tyler's eyes above me on the ceiling.

I grabbed Max's leg. We'd crashed foot to head. "Max, I know what to do. Max, wake *up!*"

15

He blinked sleepily at me as he tried to get his eyes focused on my face. "What?"

"I have a plan, Max. I know exactly what I need to do."

"Whazzat?"

"I'm going to go to LA and find Steven Tyler. And when I tell him what happened, he's going to explain *everything* to me, until it makes sense."

Then

Chapter Two: The Fun and the Fury

I started working for *Whipt!* by plan. I had been writing for my high-school newspaper, magazine and yearbook since I had arrived there. A rock-n-roll epiphany when I was on the brink of graduation had convinced me that I didn't want to do journalism; I wanted to do balls-to-the-walls *insanity.*

It took several totally crappy jobs to put together what I needed to get into *Whipt!* – namely a car to get to work with and enough black in my wardrobe to look the part. When I finally got in, *Whipt!* fit me like really good leather. *Whipt!* existed in a little bubble of bizarro, not unlike me. It was the first place I had hung in years where I wasn't the weirdest one. It wasn't just a job. It was an adventure. And a lifestyle. *My* lifestyle, and it had just been waiting for me to show up. I got hired to answer phones, type letters and greet visitors. The whole time, I was kissin' ass and takin' names.

The publisher, Blue Tingles, looked like he could be Hugh Hefner's kid. Dark hair, cut long; lots of leather suit jackets, cut long; circumcision, cut long. One day he asked me if I'd like to do a restaurant review – no promises – and I jumped at it.

I called up my best friend, Max Vermilion. Neither male nor female, a human genis with a penis. He *is* Vermilion Gallery on Michigan Avenue in Bricktown. Sometimes he shows me a dark and tender heart, a need for shelter and hope, and lets me open him gently while in my arms, to peer inside.

He specializes in a kind of soulfully artistic undead look, complete

17

with hair so blond it's almost white, and lots of black turtlenecks. And a boatload of mascara to trim out a pair of lake-water blue eyes. Every once in awhile he'd spice things up by slicking a tube of neon red lipstick over his lips.

"Max, I need your help. Can you go out to eat with me tonight?"

"It's drink-and-draw, tonight," he reminded me. That's the one night a week he closes the door to the public and opens it to a bunch of his current favorite alcohol-deficient artists and one nude model, and everybody sits around and gets tanked and doodles T&A – or P&A, depending on the gender of the model. Max provides free booze, so it's a pretty well-attended event. "Why don't you take Grandma Rose, instead?"

"Okay, forgot about it being D&D night. But Rose had her bunions ground down today and she got a couple of Valium appetizers. She'll get dingy and hit on all the waiters." Actually, a shot or two of Jack Black sounded pretty good right now. "How about if I meet you at the gallery. Freddy Gruesome gonna be there?"

Freddy Yak – no kidding, *Yak* – was Max's assistant and current semen receptacle of choice.

Max sighed. "Yes, Freddy will be there. We've been together two years, now, Eve. Accept."

"Well, I'll come by and hang for a couple of hours, then we can go to the restaurant and eat, and Freddy can babysit. We'll be back in plenty of time for you to close up. Who's the model? Anyone I know?"

Max made a small coughing noise. "I, um, think so. Remember that band, Bio-Degradable Shit? It's their lead singer. Loyola Monk."

"That skanky electric violin playing bitch? I hate her. You know that.

18

She tried to kick my ass in the bar one night because some guy she liked was hitting on me! She hit me with her fucking violin!"

Max made some noises, but they sounded more like smothered laughter than coughing. "Actually, Eve-my-love, the guy she liked was her husband, and *you* were hitting on him. As I recall, you grabbed both his ears and shoved his face into your tits. She almost wasn't able to get him out of there alive."

"Details. Anybody that would hit a person with a violin is wacked. Besides, it was still plugged in. My hair was frizzed for a week."

Now he was definitely laughing. "Okay, she's a bitch. Come hang out anyway and we can sit in a corner and do a couple of lines and snicker at her boobs. Now tell me, why do you have to go out to dinner tonight? And, does Grandma Rose have any Valium left?"

"Before we talk Valium and a free dinner, tell me what's wrong with the skeeze's boobs?"

"She doesn't have any. Compared to you, she actually has negative knobnicity. You make her look like the Meteor Crater of Cleavage, and you're the Mt. Everest of Mounds."

"That's sweet, Max. Thanks." Dropping into drink-and-draw was sounding better by the minute.

*

Vermilion Gallery was an old brick building that used to be some kind of warehouse or manufacturing business or something. It had to be about 10,000 square feet, and the interior walls were brick, too, and twisted around enough to turn the inside of the gallery into the next best thing to a maze. Which was cool for Max, because he had all kinds of hidden niches for collections by different artists. The floors were scuffed and scarred, a perfect match for the bar that Max had picked up at an auction. It was the room with the bar, set up with wooden tables, chairs and easels, that was used for drink-and-draw.

When I got there, Loyola Pain-in-the-Ass was already draped across some goof-ball plastic rock thing, hair trailing off limply behind her, nakidity on display for all to see. I walked over and looked down into her beady little eyes.

"Hey, Loyola? Bring your ukulele tonight, or you gonna let me kick your ass in a fair fight this time?"

She blinked at me, head upside down, and as recognition leaked into her eyeballs, so did fury. She started to sit up, and half-a-dozen guys screamed in shrill horror.

"Uh, Loyola, you don't want to move while you're being drawn. They really freak out. And there goes your shot at that *Bimbo Magazine* cover you've always wanted."

She hissed, but put her head back down. Some marginally sane jitterbug came running over, bitching and rearranging her hair just so, joined by one artist after another, as they waved their sketches in the air and argued about the position of every single strand. I heard a sigh from the middle of the pack, and thought it was Loyola's. Round one: Me – a trillion; Loyola – negative five trillion.

I wandered up to the bar where Freddy was gaping at Max with love in his eyes, visions of connubial bliss dancing in that Neanderthal brain of his.

Max gave me an amused look and slid me a tumbler of Jack Black

20

when I walked up to the bar. "Nice opening shot. Get all the obsessive-compulsives pissed at her. It'll take 'em an hour to work through the disturbed hair issue."

"My pleasure. Really. Table for two? Uh, three?" I amended when Freddy looked like he was going to cry. Jesus.

"Sure. Hey, Barrio, take over the bar for a few, okay?"

Barrio, who never missed D&D night, jumped behind the bar. As far as we could tell, he crashed inside the huge old train station a couple of miles away, along with a bunch of other crazy guys, but he was worth his weight in whiskey in cleaning up after an opening or a D&D. Plus, he was about ten feet tall and was instrumental in getting all the drunks poured back into their cars at closing time.

We retired to a corner table by the bar, and Max laid out some lines.

I raised my head, rubbed my happy nostrils with a knuckle, and knocked back my JB. I looked over at Max, who was holding Freddy's hand. Even the fact that they were all googly-eyed at each other didn't seem so bad.

"Hey, Freddy, I need to borrow Max for a little while tonight, 'kay?"

His lower lip came out, and he looked about fourteen. "What for?"

"Blue said I could take a shot at writing a restaurant review for the Pink Rhino, and he laid a credit card on me – cool, huh? Carl got food poisoning and he didn't give us a review for the issue that goes to press tomorrow, so we're one short."

"Wow, congrats," said Freddy. "That's really cool, Eve. Have you ever eaten there before?"

"Nah. It's a jazz and blues place. I like rock."

Max shook his head at me, sorrowfully. "Rock came out of blues.

21

You're turning your back on your roots, Oh Scary One."

I shrugged, and craned my neck to catch Barrio's eye. "Dude, three more! We're celebrating."

Barrio nodded obligingly and poured out three more shots, while Max laid out some more blow.

*

It was a little later than I planned when we finally got out of the gallery. "Hey," I said, as I fired the motor. "I just got the new Aerosmith on tape. You heard it yet?"

"Not yet. Anything good on it?"

"It's in the tape deck. Just push play. And then skip to track five."

I fished the bottle of Grandma Rose's Valium over to Max, and he wiggled an appreciative eyebrow at me. Then I concentrated on getting off the curb that had thrust itself under the wheels of my car, and we caromed away to the Pink Rhino as the opening chords of "Dude Looks Like a Lady," ripped through the car.

Couple Valium, couple sips out of Max's silver whiskey flask, couple toots out of Max's magic bullet, and I was ready to swear that old Ford Galaxy was flying instead of rolling. We kept playing "Dude" over and over again, trying to get the lyrics down, singing along, right or wrong, at the top of our lungs. I'm pretty sure that's what saved the old guy as we skidded onto Rivard Street, where the Pink Rhino waited. That or his reflexes. For an old guy, that dude could *jump*.

Once again, the curb forced itself under the wheels of the car. I hate it when that happens.

The Pink Rhino is topped with a huge, neon-Pink rhino, oddly enough. Food ranges from Creole to deep-fried Southern. The band was playing that fast, bouncy New Orleans' rock-a-boogie that was more infectious than malaria.

We took our seats and asked for menus, and encountered our first obstacle. It was one a.m. and the kitchen was closed. Pragmatic woman that I am, I ordered a couple of shots and started moving from table to table, asking people about their dinners.

I'd made it about halfway around the room, dancing as I went. Hey, free floor show to go with the music, right?

Apparently, our Jamaican-bobsled waiter didn't appreciate art. He came over and tapped me on the shoulder, interrupting a damn good shimmy. Bobsled man startled the hell out of me and I tipped forward and landed on the table with a boob in a male customer's margarita. I looked at my boob, then up at the guy, who looked like he'd just found out Christmas was coming twice this year.

Behind me, the waiter made a gurgling noise. I laughed. "Sorry about that, really. Let me make it up to you. Want a lick?"

His wife gaped and turned about seventeen shades of red, and then stood up and grabbed the hubby with one hand and her purse with the other. "You drunken slut. Herb, we're leaving." She gave me one of those looks that said, *I'd rip your throat out right now if I had a salad fork and an alibi.*

By now, the band had kind of limped to a stop, and everyone in the room was watching. The Jamaican moved to the wifey's side of the table; she was the one he was figuring for the tip.

"Oh, don't do that," the waiter sounded like he was going to cry. "Girl," he said, turning suddenly to me, "This ain't no strip club. Don't be

23

behaving like that in here. You need to go sit down."

I started laughing again. "Fuck off, buddy. I'm the customer here. Why don't you tell *her* to sit down? I'm not bothering anybody."

I turned to the other diners. "Am I bothering anyone here?"

Every woman in the room raised her hand. Christ!

The bitch fixed the Jamaican with a steely look, and he turned to me and started yelling. I started yelling back, and then the bitch joined in and started yelling at both of us. Which was pretty fun, actually, until she caught hubby Herb looking at my wet boob again. That cut it.

Before I knew what was happening, she started whapping me over the head with her purse. And it was a heavy-ass purse.

Spontaneous applause broke out from several different directions. I'm pretty sure one of those directions was Max's; he's such a shit-disturber sometimes.

It stopped when Herb grabbed his wife by the waist and hauled her out of the place by force. She looked over her shoulder to get one last shot in as she was dragged off. "If I'd known it was slut's night, we wouldn't have come." She pointed her nose in the air and let Herb finish hauling her out the door.

I turned to the bobsled waiter and regarded him sympathetically. It wasn't his fault she'd turned out to be such a bitch. I wasn't going to blame him for siding with her. Bygones, all that stuff. Plus, he was the one slinging the booze. "So, bring another shot for me and my friend?"

The Jamaican actually stomped his foot. "You horrible, horrible woman! You just got in a fight with one of my best customers. Get out! Get Out!"

He screamed like a girl. I returned to my seat, propped my feet up on the chair next to me, and grinned up at him. "Make me."

That's when they called the cops. Fuckers.

*

I ended up getting off with a warning after Max finally stopped laughing and pointed out that if I was arrested I might press charges against the bitch for assault, and she probably would *really* hate that.

I got to work the next morning with a hangover the size of a speeding freight train, plus that special feeling that comes from being whapped in the head multiple times by a suitcase-sized purse that felt like it was full of soup cans.

I had my review ready, though, and turned it in to the editor, John Blatt, before hustling off to my desk.

About two minutes later, Blatt was standing in front of my desk, waving the review I had just handed him in my face.

"What the hell is this shit? You didn't even eat there?"

I raised one eyebrow and closed one eye. Good, he wasn't twins anymore. "That *shit* is a slice of real-life experience at a one-of-a- kind, uniquely Detroit classic restaurant and club. And I have ten other people's reviews in there – hot from last night, and ten is way better than one, anyway."

He made the same kind of gurgling noise that the Jamaican waiter had the night before, and his face started turning a charming shade of pink. He looked much better that way, actually.

Before he could say anything else, Blue sauntered through the door, and snagged the review in question from the editor's hand.

25

We both waited silently while he read it. At the end, he burst into laughter. "Eve, this is the funniest damn thing I've ever read. This may be the best review ever written for *Whipt!* John, put it in. Trust me."

"Blue, I totally love you. Want a blow job or ten?"

"Star writers don't give blow jobs. They allow their adoring publishers to lay out lines for them."

"Alright then. Lines in your office after lunch?"

"Deal." He turned his back on John, who had started gurgling again, and walked away whistling. Great boss or what?

The review, by the way, was a hit, just like Blue had figured. We got more mail about Max and I visiting the Fat Rhino than any other piece in the magazine that issue.

I was moved in to the editorial department, as Blue's assistant, and got to write a piece for every issue. Blatt, the editor, never did get it, and ended up leaving to work for a suburban weekly. Blue, on the other hand, got it entirely, and frequently, which is how I turned a two-hundred-fifty word restaurant review into a featured column in just two notes. With a little help from Max, of course.

Now

Chapter Three: Let Frank Do It!

Satisfied that I knew the answer to my problems, I crashed hard and heavy. At some point, I remember Max planting a good-bye kiss on my forehead. He was finally sober enough to make the drive home to Freddie, so off he went. I wriggled out of most of the leather-wear and crawled under the covers.

"Max?" When he didn't respond, I guessed his thoughts. "You won't be able to go, will you." It was a flat statement. He couldn't get Freddie off his hip for a day, much less a couple of weeks.

He grinned from the doorway and blew me another kiss. "'Fraid not, kiddo. Got shows, artists, promos, etc, etc."

"And Freddie's head up your ass – don't forget that one, buddy."

He laughed. "I can only hope. Call me when you get up."

I closed my eyes and pulled the covers over my head. From their depths, I muttered, "Love you, Max."

"Right back at ya. Off to see the ball and chain."

I was back to sleep in one note. I didn't wake up until Grandma Rose banged on the foot of my bed with a skillet. Breakfast was served.

*

We decided that Bloody Marys would be just the thing to take the edge off the enormous hangovers we were sporting, so I mixed up a pitcher while Rosie plated breakfast. It got us a little snockered again, but it took care of Grandma Rose's hangover, so it was totally a win–win situation. Sometimes, doing the right thing just works out great.

27

Over breakfast, we talked. I explained my plan to go find Steven Tyler and demand answers to all my problems.

"You think he can do it?"

I fetched the DVD release of *Big Ones You Can Look At*, and popped it in to the DVD player hooked to the living-room TV.

Grandma Rose and I watched in silence as Tyler pouted, smirked, screamed and seduced, all with that frenetic sizzling energy, making music with those incredible, flexible, talented pipes.

I was keeping half an eye peeled for Grandma's reaction, but it was pretty hard to keep even that much focus off Tyler. When we got to the end of the DVD, I turned to her and said, "So, whaddaya think?"

She had a pensive look on her face, and had slouched down on the couch, her legs stretched out before her, ankles crossed. She frowned, and I thought, "fuck, she doesn't get it at all."

Then she asked if I would play 'Love in an Elevator', again.

"Sure," I replied, finding the first track. I kept looking at Grandma Rose, who was staring intently at the screen, as Tyler, bare-chested and wearing a long red jacket knotted with filmy scarves, engaged in wild sexual escapades with an elevator operator.

As always, it was a breath-choking sexual thrill to watch. When it was over, I paused the DVD and turned to Grandma. "Why did you want to see it again?"

She grinned. "Just wanted to see if I could have an orgasm twice on the same song. He must bring a lot of happiness to people. A *lot* of happiness."

Joy, relief. She got it. Apparently, she *really* got it. Could it be possible to have a better grandma than one that has an orgasm watching Aerosmith? I don't think so.

"I love you Grandma."

"So, when do we leave?"

I couldn't answer right away, because I was busy coughing Bloody Mary back out of my windpipe. Finally, I got control of my lungs again, and gawked. She was looking at me placidly.

"You want to go?"

"You said Max couldn't, right?"

"Yeah, but . . . "

"And you don't have a boyfriend to go with you, right?"

I spluttered some more. "Yeah, but . . . "

"But what?"

I wasn't really sure. It wasn't like I hated her company or anything, it's just she's *Grandma Rose*, for God's sake. And I hadn't had a boyfriend since I was in my teens. Friends with bennies, yes, sometimes even strangers with bennies. But no one but Max that I'd consider spending two weeks in a Honda with. But if she really wanted to go, who was I to tell her no?

"You know I'm planning on taking a couple of weeks, right? No agenda, no timetable, just a nice, leisurely cruise across country, get my head together, get to LA, find Steven Tyler and force the answers out of him."

She was still grinning. "I can bribe him with hot sex, if it would help."

That was disconcerting.

I had a sudden urge to switch from tomato-watered vodka to JB. Christ, I'd been mostly sober for hours now.

"Besides," she continued, "I can help drive when you want to get

29

plowed." The idea of Grandma behind the wheel made me shudder. I'd rather pound a brick into dust with my bare knuckles than ride shotgun to my grandmother. Or around the block. Even around the driveway was too much. Stationary without the keys was scary.

Thinking fast, I said, "I've got a stick, Grandma Rose. You don't drive manual."

"Well, actually, I can drive a stick a little. Frank's been teaching me. I have access to a car that would be perfect for a road trip. Wanna see it?"

Mystified, I let her pull me along to the garage, a place that I never went. I could see a hulking shape on one side, and when Grandma turned on the light, it morphed into a car covered by a tarp. She walked over and grabbed the tarp with both hands, like a magician about to pull a tablecloth out from under a set of fine china.

When she saw she had my attention, she yanked the tarp off with a flourish, upon which it snapped sharply up into the air, then fell right on top of her. She was sneezing and trying to dig herself out of the tarp, but I couldn't help. I was mesmerized by the fabulous piece of machinery sitting before me. A Gypsy-red 1955 Corvette convertible with a cream interior and fold-down top.

I moved absently to help Grandma Rose break free of her canvas restraints, and then ran my fingers reverently across the hood. Damn. Damn! "Jesus, Grandma, where did you get this? She's beautiful."

She was still patting her hair into place. "It's Frank's. He asked me to hold on to it for him, because the IRS is looking for it."

"Grandma, I don't think anyone in his right mind would let us take a car like this and go jetting off across country."

"That's why I'm not going to tell him, Eve," she said, giving me a skeptical glance.

Of course, silly me. How *could* I be so naive?

"It's been sitting here for nearly a year. No harm, no foul. No tell, no trouble. Now, keep your lips zipped and we'll be fine. Can I go, or not?"

I threw my arms around her. "Are you kidding? My car is the pits." It was all those damn curbs. "Road trip for two, coming right up. But I'm driving."

She made a pouty face. "Fine, if that's how you want it. But I get first dibs on Mr. Tyler there."

Over her shoulder, I grinned. "Only if you beat me to him."

Grandma may have good taste in men, but she's slow on foot.

Then

Chapter Four: Hard-headed Man

When I was little – four, maybe – my mom and dad and I lived in a little hippy commune in the Appalachians. That was after the little hippy communes in Florida, in California, in Idaho and in upstate New York.

People think that communes are all full of laid-back stoners, who hang out and bake brown bread and tie-dye shirts, which is totally, idiotically untrue. In reality, they are full of fringers and dopers, and a lot of the dopers no longer have enough brain cells to start a fire if they rubbed 'em together. The fringers, on the other hand, frequently had a brain-cell deficit to begin with.

The Appalachians are probably awesome for a summer vacation, but in the wintertime, they'll freeze your ass off. Especially if you're four years old and totally at the mercy of two crazy people – fringer mother, stoner dad. Christ almighty. Four nights out of five, they got too wasted to light whatever wood was in the little fireplace before they passed out. And they refused to trust *me* with the matches? Unbelievable.

I'd end up sleeping between the two of them, just for the warmth. Mel, my mom, would wake up and smile at me, like we were all lovey-dovey, when actually I was about ready to chew her leg off – which would have really caused a stir, as this was also a conclave of *vegetarian* hippies. No Happy Meals for me, no shit.

"Mom, can I watch cartoons?"

She was on an acid trip, always a good time to ask her stupid questions just to drive her even crazier than she already was.

32

She waved a hand in the air all around her and giggled. "Already are, can't you see, monkey butt?"

"No, elephant's ass. I can't."

"Don't call me that." She was sounding a little less giggly. Good.

"Mom, can we go to MacDonald's and get a hamburger?"

She shuddered, good little vegetarian that she was. "They kill cows for that. Kill them dead, dead, dead. Horrible cow killers."

"Take it easy, muttonchops. They don't hurt 'em or anything. Just a quick bullet to the brain. Hardly any blood oozes out or anything. Maybe a little blood, spilling around on the floor, dripping off its dead face . . . "

Mel burst into tears, and ran out of the room, mumbling something about blood dripping on her face. Ah, my work here was done. Scratch "terrify Mel" off the list of things to do today.

Now to go find dear old dad.

*

I wandered through our little village – ratty trailers, the wooden sheds we called 'homes', outhouses, and junk cars. The guys always looked fucked up, and people in town ignored them as much as possible. But the women were all pretty in their own ways, so they were the ones that got sent forth to beg for money.

In return for cash, a generous patron could get a homemade paper flower, a small book of Tao, or a blow job.

I ran into a couple of the other kids, all scrawny, all under-dressed in the winter cold, all with runny noses and wary eyes. They scattered like pigeons when I rushed up, then settled back cautiously when they realized it was just me. "Hey, you guys seen Bark?"

33

Bark, my father. Bark, the undad. I'd given up looking for anything but idiocy from him a long time ago. His nickname had been given to him by Bite, the alpha dog of this stupid pack. They all had some ridiculous kind of dog name. I'm guessin' Bite's was right on.

Bark was the same place he always was, sitting around at Bite's house, smoking dope and drinkin' Cokes and pretending he knew anything. Okay for him, 'cause that was what the rest of the guys were doing, too.

When I came in, they were all laughing hilariously. Bite had a TV, because Bite had a generator. Which made Bite half-a-light bulb smarter than anyone else in the entire commune, except for me.

They shut up when I came in, and Bark gave me a speculative look. "Hey, darlin', fetch your dear old dad a beer." I did as I was told, and looked at the TV screen with interest, but it was just a bunch of naked people doing stupid stuff. There was a dog, but not a cartoon dog, so I didn't really give a rat's ass.

"Bite, you wanna shut that down? We got us a lady in the room."

Bite looked like he was on a massively bad trip. He scowled at Bark like a madman, then grinned, and it was even scarier. Which proved I had more sense than anyone else in the room, because I was the only one who tried to leave.

"Daddy, I'm goin' to go home now."

Bark nodded absently, caught by the naked people on the screen again, but Bite moved to block the door before I could get to it.

"You're not runnin' away from the facts of life, little girl. And I'm not turning the TV off, Bark. You get over there and sit back down, and Uncle Bite is gonna explain the facts of life to you."

34

Dad looked at him uneasily. "You sure she's old enough?"

Bite was doing more of that insane grinning thing again. My stomach started tightening up into a painful ball, and I made a dodge for the door, delivering a good, swift kick to Bite's shin as I did so.

He howled with pain, and then snatched me up by the front of my coat and threw me across the room to dad, who didn't exactly catch me, but at least blocked my fall.

We both huddled together and pretended we weren't scared, as Bite settled in to light another joint and explain the birds and the bees to me, by way of a tape about the dogs and the sluts.

Bite blathered on and on about nature and free love and a bunch of crap that I didn't pay any attention to, while I pretended to be interested in the TV screen and practiced crossing my eyes. What an idiot. Everybody was nodding off, one by one, and I was getting a pretty good contact buzz just by sitting in the same room with all those losers. I was just waiting for Bite to fall out so I could make my escape.

I sneaked a look at him when he fell silent, but instead of sleeping, he was staring at me with that crazy look again. Without warning, fast as a snake, he stood up, grabbed me and stuffed me under his arm, and carried me out of the room. Just to make sure my four-year-old self wasn't going to call for backup, he put a hand over my mouth and nearly smothered me.

I remember struggling to draw in breath past his filthy fingers, the smell of sweat and dope making my head swim.

He carried me to another room, and closed the door, then laid me on the bed and lay down on top of me, hand still over my mouth. Very quietly, in my ear, he talked to me while he stripped off my clothes.

35

"I saw you watching that porno flick. You really liked it, I could tell. You like watching people fuckin'? Now we're gonna practice what was on that tape so I can see if you learned your lesson good."

He had most of my clothes off by this time, and was rubbing his hands and his tongue all over me. I was getting really scared. Tears were leaking out my eyes, and I would have been begging him to let me go if my mouth had been free. I squirmed and twisted underneath him, even though every move I made just brought more of his weight down on me.

The demon that was Bite unzipped his pants and pulled out his dick, and started rubbing it between my legs and all over my belly. He kept talking, real quiet, the whole time, saying what a slut I was, and how he knew how much I liked it. Sure – tears and trying desperately to stop what was happening are always a sign that a chick digs it.

Pretty soon, he was rubbing his dick faster and faster between my legs, and his body started jerking and twisting. There was a final convulsion, and I thought, hoped, that he had died.

No such luck. After a moment, he grinned up at me and said, "We'll have to do this again real soon, Evangeline. Real soon. And if you tell anybody what I did, you know what I'm gonna do?"

I shook my head.

He leaned real close. "I'm gonna fuckin' kill you, and that stupid cow of a mother, and your father, you freaky little bitch. So you keep your mouth shut, you hear?"

I nodded, and he took his hand off my face, and his massive body off of mine. For the first time in at least half an hour, I could breath. Jumping up, I scrambled to put on the rags that were left of my clothes, and then zipped my coat over the whole mess. He watched me the whole time.

I ran out into the living room, only to see dear old dad lying on the floor where I had left him. This time his eyes were open, and he was fucking crying. I get assaulted and scared half-to-death, and he's lying on the floor, ten feet away, feeling sorry for *himself*.

In that single instant, everything crystallized for me. A major epiphany: No one gives a fuck, and no one can save you.

I had planned on running like a rabbit back home, and telling Mel what had happened. Now, I cradled my epiphany in my heart, and marched over to the fireplace.

I walked back to the door of the bedroom, where Bite appeared to have fallen asleep. I raised the poker I held in my hand, and brought it down as hard as I could on his head. The first blow cracked his skull, and I got in a good ten or so more, before Bark finally got off his ass and came in to see what the fuss was. He wouldn't dream of crossing Bite to save me, but he'd poke his head in to see if I was bothering his buddy who had all the dope.

He stopped in the doorway and gaped. Bite's blood and brains were all over the fucking place, and I was damn glad.

"Evie, what the hell did you do here?" His voice was shaken, and he didn't sound stoned anymore.

I gave Bite one more satisfying blow that produced a sickening squelchy crunch, so that he could see the answer to his question. Then I turned and left. I gave my loving father a good crack in the leg with the poker as I passed. I still keep the poker with me as a reminder of what happened that day, and what I learned. No one gives a fuck, and no one can save you.

37

*

Bark had a fractured leg, and was blubbering like a little kid. My mom was running around in confusion, not actually doing anything, although I think someone eventually drove Bark to the hospital, where he got X-rays and stuff.

Nobody said anything about Bite and what had happened. My guess is that the guys buried Bite and covered up all traces of him, but I don't really know. The next morning, good ole mom and dad sent me to my Grandma Rose's. Mom's face was tight, and she wouldn't respond beyond 'yes' and 'no'. Bark just kept rolling his eyes like a scared horse. He wouldn't come near me.

They put me on a train all by myself, and split. The poker I refused to give up had been a major bone of contention, but in the end, I won. It was wrapped up in my suitcase and sent off into the wild blue with me.

The wild blue turned out to be Grandma Rose and Grandpa Joe. I remember walking into their front door for the first time. The house was big, and clean and there were no scary men in it. Just Grandpa Joe, who was already sick from the cancer that would end up killing him. He was thin and quiet, and I could have taken him even without a poker. I sat down on the couch and burst into tears, and she cuddled me up on her lap and let me cry. Then she fed me. It felt like someone really did give a fuck, after all.

I never saw my mother or father again. Bark took off from the commune, and no one knew what the hell had happened to him.

I talked to Mel on the phone a few times, early on, but that faded off pretty quick. Mel thought I was a monster. Grandma Rose, on the other hand, thought I was a hero. Uncle Joe just thought he needed more pain pills. Go figure.

Now

Chapter Five: Life is a Circus

Grandma Rose and I decided to take one day to pull together what we needed to, in order to be ready to leave. We packed, shut the house down, asked the neighbor to get the mail, paid bills.

Blue called me, but I was still kinda miffed at him for selling *Whipt!*, so I didn't call him back. We drove to the gallery that night to have dinner with Max and frustrate Freddie. Once we were all together, we went over to a pub in Corktown where we could grab a bowl of Irish stew and a trawler-load of Irish Whiskey.

Freddie's relief that I going away for a couple of weeks was tempered by the fact that Max had passed out at my house the night before instead of coming straight home.

"I don't think you'll really be able to see Steven Tyler when you get out there. He's a superstar. And he's sooo cute."

Max gave him a scandalized glance.

"Well, he is. That tight little butt and all that hair? Gorgeous."

Grandma Rose nodded. "That's what I think. Did I tell you I had two orgasms watching 'Elevator Love'?

I rolled my eyes. "'Love in an Elevator', Rosie-o."

"Whatever you call it. I'd go down with him in two notes."

"Me too," sighed Freddie.

Max gave him another one of those looks, but Freddie ignored it.

Just to needle Freddy, I asked again if Max would come with us. "We'd make a great threesome," I purred at Max, laying a hand on his arm

39

seductively. "Don't you think, Grandma Rose?"

She was wobbling to her feet to hit the ladies' room, and smacked me on the back of the head as she passed. "Stop teasing Freddie, Eve. He's a nice boy. And he's got good taste in men."

"Ow!"

Freddie grinned. "You're gonna spend two weeks in a car with her? I'm lovin' it."

"Bite me."

While she was gone, Max asked me to keep him posted on my trip.

"No problem, Max. I'm taking my laptop. Just check your email. I'll write you every night, I promise."

"Be careful out there in the world, Eve. And take good care of Grandma Rose. I'm very fond of her, you know."

I patted his hand. "I know, Max. I love her, too. Nothing's going to happen."

Freddie snorted.

*

Next morning was it. We loaded up Frank's convertible, I threw all my Aerosmith DVDs and CDs into a case, and stowed them under Grandma Rose's seat, along with my laptop and a portable DVD player that plugged easily into Frank's cigarette lighter.

Grandma Rose came out, lugging a cooler full of snacks and juice and stuff, along with a few bottles of hard lemonade. I cracked one to prime my pump for the drive ahead.

While I worked my way out of the city, we considered where we would go first.

40

*

The first night, we stopped in a nondescript little town in Indiana, where I got funny looks, and not much else. I was thrilled with the Roadster; she was a certified Dream Mobile, roaring down the highway and shifting smooth as cream. As a matter of fact, I'm pretty sure she drew more looks than I did.

The next morning we got up bright and early – meaning before noon – and headed toward Grandma Rose's first requested stop: Jackson, Tennessee, of Johnny and June Carter Cash fame, home of the Rock-a-Billy Hall of Fame and Museum. I belted hard lemonade while Grandma Rose wandered around and tried to convince me and our guide that she had boinked Johnny while June wasn't watching. I found that highly doubtful, if for no other reason than that June Carter looked like a woman who could take Grandma Rose in anything from arm wrestling to rocket launching. After wasting most of the morning there, we got back on the road, deciding that we'd waste most of the afternoon in Memphis.

In Memphis, the climate is mild, the Coca-Cola still comes in icy glass bottles, and there are nearly as many Elvis impersonators strolling around as there are in Vegas. We did the obligatory Graceland tour to satisfy Grandma Rose, peering at the stained glass peacocks, the scarlet love seats, the bits and pieces of Elvis Depressedly's life. When Grandma tugged me along to the gift shop to get some signature Elvis hair pins, I announced my new nickname for the King. I barely escaped the gift shop alive. Christ, those people have no sense of humor.

We crammed ourselves back into the Roadster and burned rubber out of there. One fat old broad chased us halfway down the block, and it was

41

a big block. I don't think she would have stopped at all if she hadn't slipped on an oil slick and flown up in the air, fat feet flying up over her head, giving us a great view of an ugly ass.

I shifted and hit the gas, and nearly lost it on the corner as the Roadster way overreacted when I wrenched the wheel. My heart had time for one desperate thud before we straightened out and all four tires hit the road again. Mental note to self: easy on the corners in the Dream Mobile.

The light was fading, so after we put the Elvis fanatics behind us, we started looking for a place to crash for the night. We were most of the way to Little Rock and I was on the last bottle in the six-pack of hard lemonade, when Grandma spotted a hotel from the highway named "The Hairy Bear Butte Hotel, Restaurant and Bar". The sign with the name on it was topped with a neon bear who pranced around in a hula skirt while her long blond hair fluttered. It looked a little like Cindy Bear from those old Yogi cartoons. I cut across traffic to hit the exit, flipped off the honking drivers behind me, checked to see if any of the Elvis nuts were still on our tail, and zoomed up the exit ramp.

Grandma studied the sign as we got closer and closer. "Is it just me, or does that sign say 'Hairy Bare Buts?'"

"Either way, it sounds pretty good to me," I said, happy at the thought of a hot bath, headphones and one of the bottles of Jack I had stored in my suitcase. "What's that say underneath it?"

Grandma Rose squinted up at the sign, and slowly puzzled out the words. "Winter Home of the Hairy Bear Circus and Traveling Show. Performances Nightly.

"Maybe we'll get a floor show with our meal," said Grandma

hopefully.

"You like circuses?"

"Haven't been to one for a while, but I used to love 'em."

We pulled into the parking lot and started unloading our luggage.

We stepped into the lobby, and into a different world. The ceiling was draped with canvas to look like the inside of a circus tent. There were spotlights scattered here and there, murals of excited crowds painted on the walls, and a dozen guests scattered here and there.

As we got closer, I could see that at least four of the 'guests' were actually sculptures, faces reflecting laughter, terror, surprise and sadness, respectively. Candles flickered in corners, and zippy calliope music took odd turns into threat and violence. Way cool.

We approached the check-in counter, but before we made it all the way across the lobby, three men zoomed out on unicycles and started circling around us, singing:

Welcome to the Hairy Bear,
Ne'er you saw a sight so fair.
As deadly maidens, dreaming deep,
The Rat that eats our fluffy sheep.
The hairy bear will do you right,
just don't entice his appetite!

Having reached the end of their song, the trio skidded to a stop right in front of us, and picked up our suitcases. The guy who got mine hefted it appreciatively, making the Jack bottles ring together. He gave me a wink.

43

"How many rooms do the two of you want? Two have werewolves, one has a haunt," said another, a dapper midget with a neat goatee and a straw boater. Except for the vertical adjustment and the fact that he was black, he looked like Dick Van Dyke in *Bye Bye Birdie*.

Grandma Rose looked enchanted. "One, please. And where's the bear?"

"We'll be serving dinner in the lobby in about an hour. Our hairy bear will join you there."

"Oh, my God, I really need a drink." Against my better judgment, I let them lead me away.

*

After a coffee-cup full of Jack, I was feeling a lot better about the whole thing. When our waitress walked over on her hands to take our order and write it on a tablet with her feet, I didn't even blink. And, that wasn't even the oddest thing. She was wearing a bikini, so that we could see the fierce tattoos covering every square inch of her skin, including her face.

The waitress informed us that it was Gypsy night. We had our choice of Roma chicken with Italian sausage and a side of Gulyas – a mix of corn, tomato and green peppers; Gypsy goulash; or a Romany pasta dish with artichokes and shrimp. For dessert, there was a Gypsy tart that appeared to be pretty much melted dark sugar poured onto shortbread and topped with sweet cream made crunchy with vanilla beans. It was all served with a red wine that could peel paint. When the waitress 'handed' herself back to the kitchen, Grandma Rose leaned over and said in my ear, "That'd be a tough act to pull off if you didn't have a Brazilian wax."

As dinner emerged from the kitchen, the lights dimmed and spots came up on the small stage. The curtains opened to reveal a bear in a blond wig and a full skirt, dancing on her hind legs while one of the unicycle bellboys fiddled Leo Sayer.

The ringmaster turned out to be the Dick Van Dyke aficionado. He did a short tap-dance number next to the bear, then bowed deeply and said:

"Ladies and Gentlemen,
Guys and their wives
We're here tonight
To share our lives.
Freaks and misfits,
Hucksters with pranks,
Give us your dough,
We'll show you our wanks!"

There was a great burst of laughter at the last line, and the fiddler switched from Leo Sayer to "I Wanna Sex You Up," while the ringmaster gave the bear a twirl and then started humping her. It was like watching a chihuahua hump a mastiff, and another burst of laughter erupted. The bear looked behind her and peeled back her lips; she was laughing, too. I reached into my bag for the JB I had stashed there.

The dancing bear and her ringmaster boyfriend went whirling off around the room, and the stage was taken by a man in dreadlocks who was painted white all over, including his hair. He wore a short ivory loincloth over his hips. In a deep, foreign accent, he announced himself as "Rob, the Zombie King."

45

Rob started out juggling with rolls from a nearby table. Then he hypnotized the nearest diner to keep juggling, and moved to the next table, where he juggled spoons with one hand, followed by hypnotizing another diner to keep the spoons going.

The bear and the ringmaster were still whirling around the room, and half-a-dozen amateur jugglers were tossing God knows what. My heart was pounding in time to the music, which kept getting louder and louder. The fiddler sounded like an insane man, pumping out music so fast that you could barely see his bow moving on the fiddle. It sounded like the Doors' "The End" on crack.

The Zombie King switched from juggling to swallowing swords, and started hypnotizing diners to do the same. The lights started flickering, then full-out strobing. I could feel my stomach clench. Not good; not fun anymore. Things were taking on a decidedly nasty turn, and adrenaline was sizzling in my muscles, telling me to fight or run – right *now*. Some people weren't doing so well with the sword swallowing. Several people were cutting themselves and choking on their own blood.

The dancing bear raised her head to catch the smell of it, and her lips peeled back again. This time she wasn't smiling, and she reached down and started ripping the flesh off her tiny dance partner, who screamed in agony and spurted blood.

Jugglers started dropping things, plates and cups hitting fellow diners on the head, shattering and throwing shards of glass and ceramic around the room. A candle fell over and caught a tablecloth on fire. I grabbed Grandma, and she grabbed back. I started scoping out the exits to see which one was least obstructed. One guy had a splinter of glass as large as my finger

46

lodge itself deep into his eye. He rose, screaming, and staggered around the room.

The Zombie King saw us and grinned, threading his way around his screaming, bleeding victims to get to our table. Grandma Rose got to her feet, face white as a sheet. I stood, too, and we walked forward to meet him, holding onto each other with shaking fingers.

When we were about two feet apart, the Zombie King stopped, and as the light strobed frenetically, I noticed for the first time that he had scarlet irises with vertical slits for pupils.

That was all I had time to notice, because as he reached for Grandma Rose, she launched herself at him and landed a good hard right in his belly. Before he could recover, I kneed him in the balls.

Grandma Rose kept bashing as he slid to the floor and tried to cover his head with his hands. I pulled out my Glock and aimed it straight at his crotch.

The music changed again; it sounded like Joe Perry's pounding lead for "Livin' on the Edge", and over it, I could hear the Zombie King's voice. He was breathless from the injury to his balls, and laughing at the same time. "Okay, Okay, I give up! Uncle!"

The Aerosmith clued me in. I pointed the Glock at the floor and reached down to pull Rosie-O off the Zombie King. It took a little doing. She didn't like fights, but she was tough to stop once she got going. Especially when she was winning.

As I got her back onto her feet, the lights stopped flashing, the fire went out, and all the bleeding wounded stopped crying and moaning and spurting blood. "Grandma, look!"

47

She looked around the room as the Zombie King got to his feet. He was grinning again, as he rose and bowed to us both. Behind him, all of the other diners and performers straightened up and started applauding.

He turned to face the room full of people. "May I proudly introduce to you the newest members of the Hairy Bear Circus: Rose Spivak and Eve Petra!"

There were shouts and cheers and more hand-clapping. Grandma Rose blinked and looked at me. "It was all a fake?"

"Yeah, I think it was."

The Ringmaster stepped forward and said grandly, "Repeat after me the motto of the Hairy Bear. Now and always, for you we'll care."

He cleared his throat and screamed at the top of his lungs, joined by everyone in the room:

"Ladies and Gentlemen,
Take my advice:
Pull down your pants,
And slide on the ice!"

Grandma Rose looked at the cheering, jostling crowd as a champagne cork popped. "You're sure? It was all a fake?"

"Yeah."

She started punching on the Zombie King again. This time it took three of us to drag her off.

Once we got Grandma settled down, we were passed around the room, being hugged and congratulated on joining the circus. The Zombie

King and the Ringmaster were pouring champagne and passing full glasses around the room.

The dancing bear slipped out of her costume, and turned out to be the tattooed, hand-walker waitress.

The guy with the shard of glass in his eye came over and showed Grandma Rose that it was actually a prop that clipped on to his fake eyeball; he'd lost the real one years ago in a factory accident.

Some spiked espresso, more champagne and the joint Grandma Rose dragged out and started passing around completed my decompression. The fiddler kept playing, switching over to actual fiddle tunes like "Devil Went down to Georgia," and by the end of the night, Grandma was sailing gaily around the stage in the Ringmaster's arms.

Rob the Zombie-King came and sat down at my table. His contacts were out, and his eyes were hazel, not red. "Having a good time?"

His white body paint wasn't a smooth and perfect coat. It looked like some kind of chalky whitewash, and his eyes were outlined in red. I hit the joint I was holding.

"Yeah, Yeah I am. You guys really got me, until the Aerosmith kicked in."

"We do it every time a first-timer shows up. We mostly cater to other circus folks, so it's a lot of fun when someone wanders in by accident."

"I bet." I passed him the doobie. "How'd you end up in this freak show?"

He laughed. "We're all freaks in one way or another. It just seemed natural."

The tattoo girl handed over, then flipped around to sit upright in a

49

chair. Rob passed the joint over to her, and she drew in a toke deep enough to nearly burst her bikini.

After turning it around in my mind for a minute, I said, "I don't get it. You're not a freak. That I can *see,* anyway. So why is this the place for *you?*"

"How deep do you want me to get?"

The Ringmaster had passed Grandma off to the Strong Man, and joined us at our table to listen in. Grandma was chatting a mile a minute with her new dance partner, who had a nose ring, a beard down to the middle of his chest and a silver bar the size of a baby's arm passing through his stomach.

"Deep. Try me. I'm going through a freak stage of life right now, myself."

"Well, the way I see it, we're all freaks. Sometimes it shows on the outside, sometimes only on the inside. Just like the Ringmaster has no control over his size, I had no control over the fact that I grew up in orphanages."

I thought about Bite and nodded. "Okay, I'm with you so far."

"When I was little, my mom married this guy that beat the shit out of me." He turned and showed me his back. What I had thought were uneven streaks of paint turned out to be scars that raced across his back and ended in ugly rosebuds of puckered flesh.

"Mom totally believed him that that was the way to raise a boy; she was so damn grateful to have someone to help pay the bills. And the really fucked up thing was that his dad had treated him the same way. He really thought that's the way fathers treated sons. He'd get drunk and cry while he laid my skin open with a leather belt. The pucker at the end of each scar is from his buckle."

I thought about my father, lying outside of Bite's door and crying while Bite used my four-year-old body to jack off with. "I buy it so far."

He looked me in the eye and nodded. "I think you do. I go to school, I go to other kids' homes, and I think, 'is it happening here, too?' Because if it was, everyone was pretending, and if it wasn't, what was so fucked up about me that I deserved it? I finally hit the road when I was about fourteen. I couldn't stand it anymore. Not the beatings, exactly – you can get used to anything. But the fucked-up-ness of the whole thing. And I was determined to find something better. I figured I could drown under the waves or learn to ride them. Ended up here. Old guy that did sleight-of-hand took me in. Never touched me, never asked me any questions. Never let anybody else bother me, either. People in the circus? They embrace the wild, open up to it. They let themselves be vulnerable by not covering up. That's what I was looking for. That's why this is my place."

The dancing bear-woman and the Ringmaster nodded in agreement. "It's like this," the Ringmaster said. "We have no power over most of life, anyway. Not a damn thing I could do to make myself an inch taller – or an inch shorter, for that matter. But people still acted like it was my *fault,* somehow. The difference between me and most folks is that I bow to the wild and put my energy in opening up to it, not hunkering down and protecting ourselves. We trust to luck and the rhythm of the universe. Cause we can't do it alone, that's for sure."

"I just got fucking fired," I said, leaning back. The fiddler started playing "Mama Kin," real quiet and slow. We passed the joint and listened to the music, while I told them my story.

When I was done, the Zombie King leaned forward. "What I don't

51

get is why you stayed there so long. I mean, did you expect it would just *last?*"

It was a question I had never asked myself, and I had to stop and consider the answer. After a moment, I replied. "Yeah, I think I did. All the rockers were getting older, and growing up, and we were going to take over the world. Who would have thought a bunch of calculator-heads would take it all away from us when we weren't looking? I didn't see it coming."

"And now you're stuck because you don't want to let yourself change and evolve the way the world around you has."

"I can't change. I'm . . . me. That's all."

There was some quiet laughter around the table. The Ringmaster spoke this time. "Life is change. When you stopped evolving, you got stuck. You turned yourself into a one-trick pony. And instead of accepting that life is changing, you're all hung up on how much you didn't want it to. You won't let yourself be open to it. This change will be the best thing that could possibly happen to you."

I goggled at him. "My life is ruined! How could this possibly be good?"

He winked at me. "Magic. Wait and see."

Wise-ass. He got the last word in, though. We crashed right after that, having chosen the room with the haunt. She turned out to be the spirit of an antique fortune teller machine, and when I hit the button she cackled evilly and spit out a ticket that gave my lucky numbers on one side, and said "Get your shit together," on the other. Figures. Even the fortune teller is a smart ass.

Grandma Rose's fortune said, "Your true love awaits," which made her laugh.

The haunting part turned out to be random unsettling giggles from the corner the fortune teller occupied, along with her eyes occasionally lighting up and glowing. I settled that by unplugging her.

I sent a short message to Max via email, describing our escape from Graceland and the Zombie-Horror-Circus Act. I finished up by describing what Zombie Dude and the Ringmaster had said about accepting change and the whole one-trick-pony thing. *If midgets can get it, why is it so hard for me, Max? Was I stuck? Is that why I can't get my brain around moving on to something else – because I can't accept that life has changed?*

I looked at the blue screen for a minute, then added one more line. *Fuck it.* I hit send and crawled under the covers.

The next morning I woke up and checked the plug. It was still out, but I distinctly remembered being roused out of a sound sleep several times by the fortune teller's cackle. I laughed a little to myself. Someday, I'd come back and check out the werewolves.

Then

Chapter Six: Gross Pointe Blues

Grandpa Joe lasted two more years after I arrived, before dying of cancer. I was used to taking care of adults; my relationship with Grandpa Joe fell into a comfortable routine of my fetching him things and changing the TV, and napping on the foot of his bed. He died with a sigh, and I sighed and let him go.

I was about ten when Grandma Rose married Grandpa Simon. He was a lot of fun. Like Grandpa Joe, there was nothing scary about him. He puttered around and talked to himself, and acted perpetually perplexed as to how he had wound up living with "two gorgeous gals", and let us tease him and pamper him and help him find his glasses when they were lost – almost invariably on top of his head. *He* died in a car crash, T-boned by a drunk driver who walked away unscathed. Which goes to prove that it's better to be a drunk driver than it is to be plowed into by one.

Once Grandpa Simon died, I felt more and more detached from school, from fun, the other kids; from life, basically. What was the point of trying, if you still ended up bleeding all over the dashboard on some drunk's whim?

At fourteen years old, everyone in my life that should have loved me, or that I loved, had taken off on me, except for Grandma Rose. I watched her like a hawk for signs that she was getting ready to ship me out or croak on me. I was pretty sure that everything that had happened up to that point was somehow my fault, that somehow, my mother had conceived and given birth to a monster, instead of the cute little girl she thought she was getting. I

54

started thinking about just killing myself and getting it over with. Daily. While I was pretending to listen to whatever shit was going on in the classroom, I was carefully drawing plans in my notebook for the best way to off myself. I figured I'd wait until Grandma Rose got ready to make her move, and then, *Blam!* All over for the tough shit kid nobody wanted.

I started dressing to reflect my intentions. I went for weeks without wearing anything but black. I got a Joan Jett haircut, silver nail polish, a pair of leather boots that came up nearly to the cheeks of my ass. I got pierced, and even got a tattoo.

The only good thing that happened the year Grandpa Simon died was that I met Max. He saved my life, I think, just by being.

I was walking down one of the broad central hallways at Grosse Pointe High, when I saw a slender, elegant guy who looked like a ballerina compared to the assholes that were trailing him down the hallway and calling him a fag. It was Max, although I had no idea who he was at the time.

He didn't look angry or scared or anything, just a guy with places to go. But I was close enough to see when his eyes flicked left and right and he ducked down a mostly deserted side hall.

Oh, my God, I thought. *That moron is gonna get creamed.* I looped across the hall and followed the jocks that were following him. I could tell they thought they were gonna cream him, too, once they got him split off from unfriendly witnesses. I couldn't help myself.

I turned the corner just in time to see Max turn on his persecutors and reach into the neckline of his shirt to pull out a thumb-sized silver canister on a long chain. He flipped the tube in the air and then looked at the head idiot. "Come here, I want to show you something."

55

"Is that what you stick up your ass for kicks, you stupid fag?" Nonetheless, the jerk stepped forward, and I darted around to stick a foot in his way. He stumbled drunkenly forward, off balance, and Max maced the hell out of everyone within arm's reach.

Holy shit, was it funny. One guy was gagging in a corner, trying not to puke, a couple more were temporarily blinded by the fumes. The guy who was the chief instigator was lying on the floor, tearing up like a Victorian heroine. I gave him a kick in the gut since I was standing right there.

Max raised his eyes to me. "I think we should get out of here before that stuff wears off."

"Pretty much hilarious," I offered as we walked away.

"They're idiots. Queer isn't synonymous with stupid *or* gutless."

"You took out a half-dozen jocks by yourself. I guess not."

He grinned. I grinned. I think I actually skipped, for the first time in my life. Of such things friendships are made – thank God.

*

Max and I had a couple of other unlikely bonding experiences that year. After Max got on the upside of the jocks, he developed a goofy crowd of followers that developed into our own little clique. Imagine me – child murderer, isolated, mourning rock-n-roll hard-ass – in the center of my own clique. A few of us were on the staff of the high school newspaper, a few on the school radio station, like that. Max ruled the art department. There were enough of us that we could seriously sting somebody if they bothered us. Strength in numbers and all that shit.

The jocks hated us, and acted on that hatred as often as possible. One day, not long after Max had maced the hell out of them, they cornered me coming out of the photography class lab. The guy who'd instigated all the shit with Max – Jay – was apparently still in charge.

"Hey," he challenged, stepping in front of me. "Where's your faggoty-assed boyfriend?"

"You know, Jay, there's an oxymoron in there, somewhere. You should think about that." I tried to step by him, but he shifted and blocked me.

"You callin' me a moron?"

"I don't need to. Everyone already knows you're a moron."

That earned me a slap on the head, hard enough to make my ears ring. Not good.

"You better watch your mouth, bitch. Or you're gonna regret it."

He grabbed one of my tits with a big, hurtful hand. Definitely not good.

I raised a knee, and pulled a knife out of my boot. Jay wasn't watching my hands; he thought I was trying to knee him in the groin, and he was too busy congratulating himself on his evasive maneuvers to realize that wasn't the play.

Until I jabbed the tip hard enough to make him bleed a little. He rolled his eyes, trying to see what was under his chin.

"Jay, you are such an idiot. Now, you guys all step away from me real slow, or I'll slit his throat."

"Hey," protested Jay weakly. "You can't do that."

"And you can't terrorize people and grab chicks' tits just because you feel like it. Are you really so stupid you think that I'm gonna follow rules when you don't?"

"Hey! What's going on here?" It was a teacher, and I hit the button to

57

slide the blade back into the hilt, which was shaped like a Bic.

"Oh, Jay was just lending me his lighter."

"Jay!" Shock. Their perfect jock smoked?

"Well, I guess I'll be running along, now. Jay, thanks. I'll get that bag of weed to you later."

I could still hear the teacher blustering as I took off.

The next day, copies of a full-color picture of Jay and gang, heads carefully inserted onto a photo of gay love in action, started appearing all over school. Jay became a laughing stock, and him and his homies stopped hanging out so much. Now, who do you think could have been cruel enough, and talented enough, to do something like that?

*

Then there was the night a bunch of us slid out to the gravel pit to go swimming. Blasted, of course. Gravel pits are all over Michigan, abandoned once the ground water rises up to claim them. It's a rite of passage for the grown-ups to say they're dangerous, and for teenagers to go drink beer and skinny dip in them.

"Hey, dudes, look at this!" Studderdone took an industrial-size rubber band out of his car and hung it from the branch of a tree that was suspended over the pit. He swung out, and the branch cracked and shuddered. It didn't break off, but it dropped – just enough to startle him, so that he grabbed tighter to the stretchy band instead of letting it go. *That* was a mistake, but then, Studder was a frickin' moron, so no surprise there. He crashed into the pit wall, knocking himself unconscious.

Studder disappeared under the water, then floated back up to the surface, face down, frizzy blond hair making a groady halo around his head.

I was sitting on the grass, passing a joint back and forth with Max, when Studder hit the wall. All of a sudden there's a tidal wave of people making tracks for the cars. "Studder's dead," hollered Danz, as he ran by, nearly knocking the joint out of my hand.

Shades of *I Know What You Did Last Summer*. Too wasted on sex, drugs and rock-n-roll, too squeamish, too worried about self-preservation.

Except for Max. Max jumped into the water immediately, and I ran for the tree to grab the big rubber band. Between the two of us, we got Studder out and back on dry land, where he threw up all over my boots. Sitting there, soggy and covered in beery vomit, Studder looked up at me and grinned weakly. "Fuckin' fun, huh?" Moron. Total moron.

Next week, I did an editorial in the school newspaper about what had happened at the pit and all the fuckin' bail-ass cowards that left us there. Outcast was cool with me. Being *in* was totally sick and wrong. Max and I were tighter than ever.

But I had nightmares about Studderdone dying for a long time after that – of being one of the chicken-shits that took off and left him floating face down in the water to die. Fuck the chickenshits. Fuck the cliques. Fuck thinking first.

All that anger that had been raging around the insides of the little glass box that held my heart, the incendiary hatred I felt for myself? Like a key in a lock, something clicked, a floodgate opened, and the current reversed. Just like it had when I fought back against Bite. I was alive again. I had something better than myself to rage against; I'd rage against everyone, everything else, except for Grandma Rose and Max. I was still a monster, I was pretty sure, but there were some things that monsters were good for –

like checking all the other monsters out there. And that's pretty much how it's been ever since.

Now

Chapter Seven: Emerald City Ugly

There used to be a town in Kansas that was known as Dorothy Gale's "hometown" because L. Frank Baum had spent time there when he was working on *The Wonderful Wizard of Oz*. Just to drive the point home, the nondescript little town of Corn Husk, Kansas had changed its name to Emerald City, and built a museum in honor of Baum's books, right in the building that was the basis for the real Emerald City.

Grandma Rose has a majorly skewed appreciation of literature, and loved the Oz books, so when she saw a sign on the highway for the Official Oz Museum, she told me that was where she wanted to stop next. This time we were in the right lane when the exit came up, and we sailed up the ramp like it was motocross.

Of course, not everyone is a motocross fan, so we caused a little horn-honking when we hit the surface road, but it was an opportunity to flip everybody off with gusto, so it was still fun.

The museum was right on the main drag – which was actually called Yellow Brick Road, to my consternation – so we stopped there first, and ponied up the cash to enter. I poured a hard lemonade into a lidded coffee cup and stuffed a pint of Jack in the thigh-high boots I was wearing, and was ready to face as many flying monkeys as it took to please Grandma Rose.

When you step into the museum, you actually step into a replica of Auntie Em and Uncle Henry's place. Ugh. It's all gray and doilied, and there's a woman in there that looks like Auntie Em who points out different Oz artifacts in the room while using a voice sharp enough to scrape paint off a

61

barn.

A short walk forward puts you in a moving hallway that shakes and rattles like a tornado is attacking. Flashing pictures of the bike bitch/wicked witch flash on the window screens.

And then . . . you're in Oz. Colorful, brightly lit, populated with a somewhat reduced number of Munchkins, but what the hell.

There's a yellow brick road that you follow to hit all the points of interest. There's an assortment of Munchkins, Winkies, green-tinted aristocrats, winged monkeys and Dorothy's fellow adventurers standing by to answer questions and perform little routines from the film, or to encourage visitors to visit the gift shop.

Ho-fucking-hum, and I had killed off most of my lemonade. By the time we hit the gift shop, I was about ready to find a place where we could grab a meal, a hot bath and dig out a fifth to crash with.

Grandma Rose had finally settled on a pair of ruby-red bedroom slippers and some flash hairpins that spelled out "Oz" in rhinestones. Now we were standing in line to pay for them and debating where to eat and find a place to sleep.

The Munchkin working the gift counter was as dark as a Nubian Queen, done up in purple leopard skin and a big, flowery hat with purple feathers. She looked up and smiled. "There's only one place to eat while you're in Emerald City, ladies."

"Where's that?" Rose asked. Obviously, she wasn't quite as done with Oz as I was. I was starting to think I needed to get us out of here before a fuckin' tornado carried us off permanently.

"Emerald City Cafe, of course. My sister works there. It's right across the street."

My plan had revolved around convincing Grandma Rose that it was time to put the Emerald City behind us. Why can't people mind their own frickin' business?

I looked down at her with a scowl. "Hey, as long as we're talking, what the hell kind of Munchkin are you? I don't remember anyone black or anyone dressed like that, either. You look like Henrietta the hooker Munchkin."

She gave me a sardonic look. "I'm a ghetto Munchkin, bitch. Good enough for you?" She put Grandma Rose's change on the counter and the gift bag in Grandma's hand.

"Next!"

I considered poking her with a Limited-Edition, Rhinestone-Encrusted, Genuine Reproduction of the Wicked Witch of the West's Wand, but obviously ethnicity was a hotter topic in Oz than I previously thought, so I let it go. Plus the Elvis riot was still pretty fresh in my mind. God knows what the people in line behind us might do if I poked a Munchkin.

Of course, Grandma Rose was delighted to extend her visit to Oz over dinner, so we walked over. The interior looked, amazingly enough, like a restaurant plucked from the Emerald City – and not the upscale part. There were cheesy murals on the walls depicting scenes from both the movie and the books. Tables were full, and I was craning to see if there was a table tucked in a corner somewhere that every other starving person had overlooked.

No such luck.

I considered trying to talk Grandma Rose into leaving, but she had a pre-pouty look on her face, and I knew it wouldn't do any good. I sighed, trying to calculate how long it would be before I could access the pint stuck in my boot, when someone touched my arm.

I looked down to see a woman smiling up at me from a nearby table. She weighed at least three hundred pounds – although possibly fifty of that came from her glammed-up bouffant hair, and another ten or so from her makeup and fake eyelashes. She was wearing a full-length dress as big as a tent, in a bright, bright blue taffeta, with a jeweled bodice and silver tissue lame at the sleeves and the neckline. Her tits were bigger than my head. And to top it all off, she had a huge feather boa wound around her shoulders in the same shade of electric blue as her gown.

She gave a little wiggle, and I realized that *she* realized she was boggling my mind – and it made her really, really happy.

"What do you want?" I said. Everyone I'd met here I was looking down on – even the people that were *grande* size.

"You two can sit here, if you want. I've got plenty of room."

Before I could formulate a polite "fuck no," Grandma had seated herself. Jesus Christ! I took a seat.

Grandma picked up a menu and said, "I'm Rose, and this is my granddaughter, Eve. We're on our way to LA to meet Steven Tyler. Eve's agenda is of a more metaphysical nature, but I just want to bang him." That said, she calmly turned to her menu.

I burst out laughing and so did our impromptu hostess.

"My name's Twinkie," she said.

"You're kidding."

"Nope, mom named me and the other kids after yummy pop culture

64

staples. I'm Twinkie, my sister's name is Licorice. We call her Lick, though, mostly. And we have a brother named Quisp. Crunchy *and* sweet." She looked at me and batted her eyes.

"I think your sister got the best end of the deal, considering."

"Barely. Mom almost named her Ho-Ho."

"You ever have kids?"

"One daughter."

"What'd *you* name *her*?"

Twinkie shuddered. "Not after snack food, I'll tell you that. I named her Pixie."

"Uh-huh." I picked up my menu and sent pity vibes in Pixie's direction, whatever it might be. "What about Pixie *sticks?*" I inquired. By the look on her face, that had never occurred to her before. Grandma slapped my arm and distracted her by asking about what was good on the menu.

Within a minute, Grandma Rose and Twinkie were chatting about what to have for dinner, and laughing about the names of the entrees. There was an Emerald City salad, featuring a lot of green stuff, like romaine lettuce and avocado and Green Goddess dressing. There was green tea and Flying Monkey stew and rainbow sherbet. There were sandwiches named after cast and main characters.

The Ray Bolger was fried ham on rye, the Cowardly lion was chicken salad on pita, and about a thousand other frou-frou variations on corny. I poured some whiskey in my tea when no one was looking, then felt a nudge on my thigh and realized Twinkie was holding her own glass under the table and shaking it to indicate she wanted some, too.

A waitress finally drifted our way to take our orders. She looked really, really familiar. Meaning, she was about four feet tall, dressed in purple leopard print, and was wearing a big beflowered and befeathered hat. "Hey, we met your sister earlier – over at the gift shop, huh?"

She shot me a suspicious look. "You aren't one of those idiot white bitches that think they're so smart pointin' out there's no black Munchkins, are you?"

"Definitely not," I said, hoping if I lied really well she wouldn't spit on my food before she brought it out. It occurred to me that there were a lot more midgets in the world than I had realized before, and they all seemed to be a little . . . sensitive.

"Christ on a crutch," she said in disgust, "I'm the one that's gotta live with her when you people fuck with her head. What's the matter with you, anyway? You dress like you're married to one of them old Duran Duran guys!" Then she snatched up our menus like she thought we were gonna steal them.

The idea that anyone one, anywhere, on the entire planet would look at me an associate me with Duran Duran was unthinkable. They were the wimpiest-ass band of the Twentieth Century. I thought seriously about kicking her ass while making her listen to real rock and roll, but I wasn't sure how Grandma Rose would feel about that. So I kept my butt in the chair, and poured another shot into my tea.

I looked at my companions. "Duran Duran? Do I *look* like I would touch a Duran with a ten-foot pole?"

Grandma Rose didn't bother to answer; Twinkie twinkled, and I poured another shot for her, too.

*

When we were done eating, I walked up to pay the cashier at the front of restaurant, while Grandma Rose and Twinkie went to the ladies room. The cashier looked me over, taking in the spectacular boots, leather shorts and vest, silver jewelry and belt with contempt, then said, "you the one sitting with the Big Blue Whale?"

I gave her a once-over myself. "I'd rather be a whale than look like I crawled out from under a house, witchy-poo." Just as she opened her mouth to make another smart-ass comment, Twinkie and Grandma Rose walked up, and she snapped her teeth together with enough force to rattle her brain.

She slapped the change into my hand with enough force to rattle *my* brain, then hollered, "Next!"

The help in this town sucked.

*

Turned out that Twinkie and her brother and sister ran a hostel for practitioners of alternative sexuality on the outskirts of town and she invited us to stay there. "We don't have anybody coming in for a couple of days. You'll love Quisp – he really runs the place."

Grandma Rose wrinkled her nose. "That one of those pay-for-play places? Because I don't do sex for money."

"No, no, no," exclaimed Twinkie. "It's just a place to stay for people who don't fit into the . . . mainstream."

As emphatically as she had spoken, it didn't quite eradicate the horrific picture in my head of Grandma Rose hooking for cash.

Then Grandma said. "Well, good. Unless you have discounts for seniors, or something. Because a girl's got to watch her pocketbook." I hit the pint of Jack and then passed it to Twinkie.

After she got the terms of the stay ironed out, Grandma was delighted to sleep at a 'sex hotel', and I had the Glock, so we hopped into the roadster and followed Twinkie to the Center for Original Love in the dwindling light.

The center was a beautiful Victorian painted a pretty yellow, with white trim. There was a tasteful wooden sign in the yard that announced its name in old-fashioned hand-lettered splendor.

"If you don't mind climbing stairs, you can have the cupola room on the second floor," Twinkie offered as we pulled up and got out of our cars.

"Cupola? You mean that turret thingee? Turret rooms remind me of castles. Do you have a dungeon, too?" I was feeling pretty cheery. Grandma and I had finished off the pint on the way over, and it looked like I had escaped from Oz after all.

"Well, we *do*," said Twinkie, apologetically, "but Lick would have to invite you to go down there. It's kind of her own private playground."

I started to laugh, then the front door opened and an extra-large dominatrix with black-cherry lipstick and hair scraped back into a painfully tight ponytail stepped out, tapping a small whip on her palm.

"That's our Licorice," said Twinkie, then called, "Lick, I brought home some new friends. They're on their way to LA to hook up with . . . some famous guy. I thought we could give them the second-floor cupola, if you don't mind. They really are straight; they just need a room."

Twinkie climbed the stairs with us in tow, as Lick broke into a broad grin. "Friends of yours are friends of mine!" She looked us over and her brow creased slightly. "You're *straight?*"

If Lick didn't approve of better living through chemistry, this could

68

work in my favor; I could get out of here and get some nice, anonymous hotel room after all. I pointed at Grandma. "She takes Valium and smokes pot. She's a dope *fiend*."

There was an offended snort from Grandma Rose, but it was drowned out when Twinkie and Lick started laughing.

"I meant, you're sexually straight," Licorice clarified. "You know. Not a couple?"

I had an inkling of how Licorice lived up to her nickname. "This is my grandmother, for God's sake," I replied.

Lick winked at me. "You'd never guess how naughty people can be. Come on in. This is Xem, my slave."

A young man in black leather pants and a black cloak lined with red silk stepped forward. His bare, hairless chest gleamed whitely. He glanced at Licorice for permission, and when she nodded, said, "Hi. I'm Xem," as he put his hands together and dipped his head.

"Xem, take the ladies' bags up to the second-floor cupola room," said Licorice. He nodded and picked up our luggage, then headed for the stairs.

Twinkie moved over to a wet-bar set-up in one corner of the lobby. "Would you like a drink?" she asked. "I owe you a couple," she added, giving me a wink.

"Hey, Twink, is that you?" It was a man's voice from somewhere back in the house.

"Yes, honey, I'm home. Want a drink?"

"Love one," was the answer, and a completely hairless man with an elven face and a sparkling crystal embedded in his forehead sauntered into the room. His eyebrows were painted on in a stylized arch. He wandered over

69

to give Twinkie a lingering kiss on the mouth and to squeeze her dirigible-sized buttocks.

She pinked up, then cleared her throat and introduced the man with his hand on her ass as Quisp, the third leg of their snackfood-sibling love triangle, as slender and elegant as they were gargantuan. Then she got back to the important stuff. "Eve, you're a Jack Daniel's gal, right? Do you want it straight, on the rocks or with a splash of soda?"

"Straight up, with a soda on the side, if you don't mind."

"Rose?"

Grandma Rose leaned back on the sofa and sighed with happiness. "Something green, I think. How about a vodka rocks with a dollop of chartreuse?"

While Twinkie was dealing our drinks, Quisp had wandered over to French his other sister and give Xem a lingering embrace. When he saw me looking, he grinned. "I'd kiss him, too, but I *know* where his mouth has been. My sister's very naughty."

Then Quisp's eyes lighted on Grandma Rose and he smiled broadly. "Under the spell of the Emerald City, young lady?"

"Totally," replied Grandma Rose.

Quisp took his glass from Twinkie, and came over to sit down on the floor, baggy pants and beautifully embroidered Nehru jacket fitting in perfectly with his tailor's pose. He took a swallow of his drink and then set it on an end table and reached out to pull off Grandma Rose's running shoes.

To my amazement and hers, he took one of her feet in his hands and started massaging it. I swear, her eyes rolled up in her head in bliss.

Finishing with her left foot, he picked up her right and repeated the performance. When he was done, he looked at me and raised an eyebrow. "What do you think?"

I looked right back. "Have you now, or ever, had bizarre fantasies about a grandmother-granddaughter ménage-á-trois?"

He laughed. "Maybe one or two. Does that count against me?"

"Not as long as you know it ain't gonna come true tonight."

Twinkie came over with her own drink and sat down on the couch to watch.

"I'm totally overwhelmed just sitting at the feet of three beautiful women at the moment. I can't imagine anything more fulfilling."

He pulled my foot into his lap and unzipped my boot, then tugged it off gently. Out fell the pint of Jack. Then he pulled off the second boot and my Glock slid out. Quisp picked it up without a word and handed it back to me.

I put it in my bag with the pint. "You guys mind?"

Twinkie looked at Quisp and shook her head. "Nah. Live and let live, that's our motto. Really." She pointed over to the doorway we had come in by. Sure enough, in curvy purple script, "Live and Let Live," was lettered over the arch.

By then, Quisp was massaging my instep, and I was pretty much speechless for a little while.

*

While Quisp was bonding with us over our arches, Licorice had been moving around the room, setting alight a small fire in the pretty fireplace, dimming the lights a little, putting on some music. It was barely a whisper, and it took me a few moments to realize that I knew that tune. It

71

was an all-strings version of "Don't Want to Miss a Thing," to my surprise.

Tyler was speaking to me, I knew it. I just had to figure out what the message was.

I tipped my head back up off the back of the couch, and noticed that Licorice had sat down in a big wingback chair, and Xem was sitting on the floor at her feet, her hand curled lazily in his hair. The black liner he wore under his foxy eyes was vaguely Egyptian, a thick line that curved gracefully upward and tapered to a sharp point. His lipstick was the pretty shell pink usually only found on fourteen-year-old girls and Barbie dolls.

"Hey," it occurred to me, through the fog of Jack Daniels and happy feet, "how come Xem doesn't do the foot massages? Isn't that more in keeping with the whole slave thing?"

Quisp grinned, and on his forehead the crystal glittered like it shared the joke. "He'd enjoy it too much, and for all the wrong reasons. He gets a lascivious delight in being humiliated and debased. He'd have a hard-on as big as Hawaii. It would be all about him, and he'd suck your energy right out of your soles. Me? I just like to see people feel good when they're here."

"I wouldn't mind," said Grandma. "And Evie could use a little sole sucking. She's had a really bad couple of weeks."

"What happened?" asked Twinkie and Quisp at the same time.

Even Lick and Xem were paying attention. So I dragged myself up from my semi-crashed position on the couch, and told them my story.

Quisp listened intently from his spot on the floor, never letting go of my feet. It's funny how a foot massage can pull stuff out of you; they got the full scoop.

When I was done, Xem whistled.

"Think it's heavy shit, huh?" said Quisp, turning to him. Xem nodded.

"I think there's a lesson there," Quisp continued.

"What kind of fucking lesson?" I asked, interested in spite of myself.

"A lesson in humility," he said. Not so interesting after all. But by then he was on a roll.

"Humility sucks," I replied. "Humility is for assholes who can't stick up for themselves."

Quisp grinned. "That's not what Don Juan says."

"The sex guy?" Maybe it was slightly interesting.

"The Yaqui Indian guy," he clarified.

Yawn. "What does he say?"

"He says that true warriors are humble. And that humility doesn't come from bowing down in front of other people, but from not letting others bow down in front of you."

That took me a minute to untangle. "You mean, treat everybody like equals?"

Quisp nodded.

"Receptionists, too?"

Quisp nodded.

"That's totally fucking asinine. I thought you were going to say something intelligent."

He squeezed my foot gently. "When you start thinking you're more or less important than someone else because of things you *do*, or stuff you *have*, it gets your perspective all out of whack. The stuff and the doing takes the place of the *person*, and all of a sudden, you loose your stuff, your activity or your talent, and you feel like you've lost yourself. But you're right here, Eve. No one can take *you* away from you."

Twinkie and Lick were nodding.

"It sounds fucking silly to me," I said. I'd heard people spout this crap before, natch, and it hadn't made any sense to me then, either.

"I think I'd like to go check my email and see if Max wrote me back yet," I said, standing up and pulling my foot out of Quisp's grasp. Lick sent Xem to show us where our rooms were.

*

Max had written me back: *Sorry I wasn't there for the Graceland bit, sounds like fun. I miss you, of course. Have you heard from Blue? He showed up here asking about you. I gave him your cell number. Did I tell you about the show coming up?*

After a lot of blather about Freddy and the gallery, he concluded:

You should take me to the circus sometime, Eve. I agree with the Zombie dude that it was time for a change. Can't wait to see what happens next. Talk to you tomorrow, Max xx

I replied and told him about our trip to Emerald City, the African-American Munchkins, and Twinkie & Lick's House of Pain. *The amazing thing*, I wrote, *is that they're so fucking happy. How do people do that?* I took my fingers off the keyboard and looked at what I had written.

Twinkie had given us Pixie's phone number; I looked at the card with Twinkie's daughter's name and number on it while I thought about what I wanted to tell Max next.

Pixie was going to Cal State and lived right outside of LA. "Call her when you get close," Twinkie instructed me. "She can put you up and help

74

you find what you're looking for."

I finished up by telling him about the conversation I'd just had with Quisp: *Did you ever hear of this other Don Juan guy? He sounds a bit cracked to me. But it also makes sense, kind of. I don't know if Blue called or not. I've had my phone turned off. I don't really want to talk to anyone but you and Rose right now. My brain hurts. Love, Eve*

Then

Chapter Eight: Concert of the Century

I was jazzed. Jazzed on booze, jazzed on dope, jazzed on rock. Steve Tyler's rock. Joe Perry's rock. The way notes glistened as they slid from Perry's guitar when the band did "Dream On." A hot gush of union with the eighty-thousand people swaying with me in the stadium, singing the same song. People who look at rock-n-roll from the outside without getting it, talk about the goofy lyrics, or about how raw the band is, and miss the whole point. Rock-n-roll connects. It connected us that night. The power was in the union that pulled us together.

Max was on my left, and a stranger was on my right. I looked at her, the girl next to me, and she had tears pouring down her face. She looked like a prom queen, with smooth skin, smooth hair, smooth, glossy clothes. All smooth, a smooth that I already knew at seventeen would never be mine. I didn't need it. I reached over and stroked her cheek, she looked at me and sobbed and I kissed her.

She kissed me back, passionate tongue, a moan that I couldn't hear, but could feel thrumming from her throat to mine. Then we smiled, wet smiled, her red, red lipstick on my lips, slick slick tears. We turned back to the band, the Gods, the music. I wasn't a virgin – not by a long shot at that point – but I definitely was a freak. I wanted to be a God, and that was the moment that put Godhood in my grasp.

The music snicked the key in the lock, and everything in my head changed. Sex, drugs and rock-n-roll did their thing. Purpose roared through me. I didn't want to live on the edge; I wanted to dance on it, swing from it,

76

tipped in crazy ass-kicking balance while the pit gaped below.

I kissed her again, on fire with need for a hundred different things. Red, I called her in my head, because of her lipstick. I never did learn her name. Red and I exchanged wet, luscious kisses, and at the end of the concert Max caught a ride with a friend he'd run into there, and I went home with Red.

We licked each others' sweaty flesh with fiery tongues, all slick young skin and juicy heat. I slid down her body, nipping at her breasts with my teeth and then sucking on her nipples until she fisted her hands in my hair and forced my head lower. Her belly curved gently where it dropped away from her hipbones, and I growled and tugged at her belly bar and made her laugh.

Then I slid the rest of the way down, the place she really wanted me to be, and found her clit with my tongue. Beautiful juicy explosion on my mouth! I gorged myself, and when she came, I didn't want to stop. She had to fist her hands in my hair again to pull me away. I was panting and ravenous, and it wasn't until she flipped me over on my back that I remembered there was another song to this dance.

She kissed me, slow and happy, and licked her cum off my face. When she started the languid trip down my body with her tongue, terror gripped me. I actually shuddered. What the hell was this? I'd proved a long time ago that I wasn't afraid of sex – hell, I fucked like a guy, as often and as varied as I could get 'em – but gorgeous red lips sliding between my legs scared the shit out of me.

The really weird thing was, I could feel the orgasm building inside of me, and I knew I was ready to explode the moment she touched me. But

77

another knowledge drowned out the rest. If I had an orgasm with Red, it would kill me, kill my amazing purpose, I knew it.

I jumped out of bed and started jamming on my clothes.

"What's wrong?"

"I gotta go."

That was the only thing I said, and clung to it like a mantra until I was out of the apartment and back in my beat-up Galaxy 500. My body was still being wracked by alternate currents of sexual excitement and terror that I would lose that feeling of absolute *rightness* that had settled on me like royal robes earlier that night.

As my brain started working again, I tried to figure out what the hell had happened and why purpose had collided with pleasure hard enough to bust bricks. But the sense of purpose was roaring triumphantly in my ears and making it impossible to focus on anything else. Hurt like hell, but impossible to resist.

*

I had filled Max in on the whole concert thing, from the dizzying sense of purpose that had flooded me to the misfire with Red. We were on our way to the Electric Light Lounge on Michigan Avenue, our favorite campy bar in the days before we turned legal. They had a plastic dance floor that jounced and bounced while we danced and throbbed with light from underneath.

"You choked in the clutch because you could have loved her, and an orgasm with her would have meant something besides a zipless fuck. Caring about someone else would have fucked you up."

I denied it, but I had a sneaking suspicion that there was something

78

to that idea. When I had been lying on that bed, and Red was easing her way between my legs, I felt more vulnerable than I had since I was four. I could feel all my tight shell – one I'd grown carefully over years – start to crack. Fuck, did that hurt. It redoubled my determination never to let anybody in there, except for Max and Grandma Rose. They had both snuck in somehow, when I wasn't looking.

Hours later, we were dancing our asses off, and suddenly Max leaned in and yelled, "What's your pit?"

"Fuck you talkin' about?" I yelled back.

"You want to dance over the pit. What's in your pit?"

"Dunno. Normal, I guess. Giving up. Fitting in. Pretending. That's what the *purpose* is about. I'm never going to do any of those things. You have a pit?"

The music stopped at that moment, leaving me screaming into roaring silence. Max grinned at me, and I cleared my throat.
He leaned in and said quietly into my ear, "My pit's about the same as yours, I guess. It's full of pieces of myself that I gave up to fit in. Sharp as glass, hard as iron."

We had reached our table, and I grinned at him. "Let's get really drunk and celebrate."

"Sure. What are we celebrating?"

"That we know what's in the pit."

Now

Chapter Nine: Ridin' the Peace Train

After we left the Emerald City, we ambled west toward Rock Head, Colorado. Grandma Rose's AAA book said it was the Cantaloupe Capital of the United States. With luck, there would be a major volcanic explosion shortly before we arrived, completely destroying the county fair that was supposed to be happening that very weekend. But I didn't hold out a lot of hope. More likely than a direct meteor strike, maybe, but not by much.

And Grandma Rose has this sneaky luck vibe that manifests when she really, really wants something. I figured odds were that we wouldn't be struck by lightening on the way there, either.

Grandma had dug up yet another doobie courtesy of Frank, and we were passing it lazily back and forth as we went. I wasn't sure whether or not I really liked so much empty green space, but Rosie-o was thrilled, and that was good enough.

Until we noticed the smoke coming out from under the hood.

"Jesus! The car's on fire or something."

Grandma peered through the windshield. "Are we going to blow up?"

"How the hell should I know? I've never set a car on fire before."

Grandma Rose squinted at me suspiciously.

I made a deal of crossing my heart as I steered the roadster over to the shoulder. "I swear. At least, not that I remember. I haven't set anything on fire in months, except for Loyola's desk. And I put it out for her right after."

When I shut the car off, it made a horrible rattling sound and then settled into a steady hiss that sounded like steam leaving a kettle. Frickin' radiator. I turned to Grandma Rose. "Did they have radiators in 1955?"

Before she could do more than flick me an astonished glance, I answered my own question. "Never mind. Of course they did. If they didn't, someone would have specially installed one in this car, just so it could totally fuck up and rape my fucking day!"

Grandma grinned. "That's my girl. Don't let the little stuff get you down." Still chortling, she moved off to grab a seat in the shade of some humongous tree.

"Yeah," I muttered, but not real loud. "Your dentures blow up in your mouth, you'll be singing a different tune." Then I called out louder, so she could hear. "Hey, you know of any fucking parts stores for a '55 Corvette in the closest twenty or so states? 'Cause I'm thinking we'll end up having to send to Japan or something."

She waved a hand at me and grinned more.

I smoked a cigarette and stomped around for a while, waiting for the hood to cool off enough to lift.

I was trying to unscrew the still-steaming radiator cap with a pair of black panties, when a van pulled up behind us. I hoped it wasn't the guys from *Deliverance*, because it was the first vehicle we had seen since the radiator blew, and I was fully intending on us catching a ride with them.

The van was an old one, with a big yin-yang sign painted on the side. A blond-headed girl, with watercolor paint drifting across her face in soft shades of green and blue that mirrored clear, compelling eyes, leaned out and folded her hands together like she was praying. "You look like you could use some help. Want a ride somewhere?"

81

Her hair was the radiant color of white gold, and combined with the face paint, she was a study in sunlight and shadow. Behind her, the bare-chested kid in the pilot seat was nodding and smiling. "We have a tow strap, so you wouldn't have to leave the car behind."

Together, they didn't look as old as the roach clip I jammed in my pocket while I was ranting and raving.

"Where you guys headed to?"

They smiled some more, like my question was the punchline to a joke.

"Wherever Willow decides we should go," said the boy complacently, nodding at the girl.

"You're Willow?" I asked the girl.

She nodded. "And my companion is Lake." Cool, formal, and still managed to be friendly. "We were going to hook up with a bunch of people at the cantaloupe festival," she offered. "But we could go somewhere else. It's all cool."

They sounded stoned. "Are you guys high?"

More smiling and head bobbing. "We're pure. We treat our bodies as the Goddess intended."

Good thing I'd put that roach clip away. "Could we get the car fixed in Cantaloupe town? I think the radiator's blown."

"If the Goddess wills," said the girl. "If not, we'll go somewhere else till we find the spot that was meant to be."

I doubted I could last any longer than the trip to Rock Head before I whacked these guys in defense of my sanity, but before I could express how much I didn't think this would work, Grandma Rose yanked the side door

82

open and hopped in.

Done deal, show over. Lake hopped out of the van, and I noted that he was wearing a sari kind of skirt deal in a bright print, tied around his waist. When he saw me looking, he ran an affectionate hand down the material and smiled. "Willow made it for me. I wanted to get more in balance with my womanliness."

"Grow a set of tits."

He laughed. We worked together to get the tow rope on.

*

Willow didn't drive, so I piloted the van, while Lake rode in the convertible to do the brakes and whatever else you do in a towed car. I suspected he was back there making engine noises and pretending he was Mario Andretti, but it put me in control of the van, so I wasn't going to complain. Much.

About halfway there, I looked back in the side mirror to see Lake standing straight up – with his feet on the driver's seat, I'm sure – arms outstretched, windsurfing. His mouth was open wide, and I guessed he was either singing or howling at the top of his lungs.

I cut the wheel sharply, and it knocked him on his ass in the passenger seat. Willow looked at me with those amazing eyes.

"Pothole."

She didn't say anything, but I had a sneaky feeling that she knew I was lying.

We drove in silence for several minutes, then Willow turned to me. "I would be very interested in what brought you and Rose to Rock Head, if you feel like telling me."

I hesitated, then shrugged to myself. Why the hell should I care what a couple of new-age Goddess worshipers thought about my life? I took a breath and told her my story.

When I was done, she sighed, a long, attractive liquid sigh like music. "You choose a dark pair of glasses to look at life with, Eve."

"What the hell does that mean?"

"I mean, your perspective on life is a dark one. And you've been through a lot. It's hard to imagine how you get by from day to day, as much as you make yourself struggle."

"Hey, I'm not the one painted blue, traveling across the country with a guy in a skirt."

She laughed. "We have a good time. We roll with whatever happens, and don't waste time and energy on anger or sadness. We put everything into the hands of the Goddess, and live with the idea that even if it seems bad at the moment, there is a good intent hidden inside everything that happens to us."

"That's the stupidest thing I've ever heard. You just haven't had enough time to have anything bad happen to you yet. You're still practicing for having a real life," I accused.

Willow turned eyes on me that snapped with energy. "I watched my mother die of cancer when I was eleven and I spent the next seven years in foster care. Lake and I lost a baby last year, just weeks before it was due to be born. I still think about our baby, talk to her, pray for her, every day. Don't tell me I don't know about pain and sorrow and grief, because I *do*."

Her shoulders relaxed, and she smiled again. "I do know. But I'm not going to let things that I can't do anything about keep me from enjoying the

84

things I can do. I refuse to focus on the negative, on revenge and unfairness and meanness. That just gives it more power."

"It still sounds stupid. How can choosing to look at life one way or another change what happens? It can't, so how you look at it can't really make any difference."

"Because you miss all the wonderful things that way. It's like you're sitting in a house surrounded by beauty and occasional ugliness. But if the only window you choose to look out is one that's all grimed up, framed with money and pride and ego, you can't see the beauty. And if you don't become willing to move to another window, that's the only view you're gonna get. What window are you looking out of, Eve?"

"The one that looks out on the truth," I said. Fuck all this change your attitude/change your life bullshit. She could sell it on PBS, if she wanted to, but I wasn't buying any. "You guys are crazy."

Willow laughed, a pretty, carefree sound. The little bitch sounded happy as hell. She gave me a gay smile. "And what you believe is making you so much happier?"

I sulked the rest of the way into Rock Head.

Then

Chapter Ten: Church of the Same Ole, Same Ole

Right at the end, when Grandpa Joe was really sick, I decided I wanted to go to church. I'd never tried church before. Bite had thought churches were stupid, and that was enough for Mel and Bark. The fact that Bite had hated it was totally enough to make me want to go.

Grandma Rose didn't try to talk me out of it, although, looking back, it has to be one of the weirder things I've done. She didn't go with me, but that was okay. I understood she didn't want to leave Grandpa Joe alone in the house in case something happened.

I called around a few churches, got the hours and stuff, and decided I wanted to try The Church of God's Blessings. *We could use some blessing,* I remember thinking at the time. *Might as well go straight to the source.*

I combed out my hair, put on a dress and my best shoes, and walked over to the church on Sunday morning. I was six, and I was ready for my soul to be saved. As long as it involved healing Uncle Joe, too.

The pastor was standing at the door, shaking hands with people as they came in, and he stopped me as I went past. "Hello, there, little girl. I don't remember having seen you here before."

"That's because I haven't been here before," I said.

"Where are your parents?"

"I think they're in a commune in Florida or something. Do I need parents to come in? It didn't say anything about parents in your Yellow Pages ad." Even at six, I was a hell of a researcher.

There were several other grown ups who had stopped to listen to this exchange. He looked at them, then leaned over to look me in the eye. "The worship of God is a very serious business, little girl. Do you think you can behave in here and be quiet and respectful? Because if you act up and act foolishly, God will *get* you!"

He had half shouted the last part, then he and the other adults started laughing. A nasty picture of how Bite had 'gotten' me appeared in my mind. I looked the pastor in the eye. "I thought God said 'suffer the little children to come unto me'. Why would he try to hurt me if I'm already here?"

The pastor huffed and straightened up. He didn't look nearly as friendly in person as he had in his picture. "Well, if you're really serious, you better hurry up and go on in. God doesn't like slackards and latecomers, either."

I started to open my mouth and tell him what God had said about prodigals, but he pushed me along with a hard hand on my shoulder and I got caught up in the flow of people entering the church.

I was directed to 'Sunday School' down a linoleum corridor, where a bunch of other kids approximately my age were sitting quietly in folding metal seats. I thought it was some kind of weird game at first, but they were all just being *quiet.* It creeped me out. When the teacher's back was turned, the girl sitting next to me leaned over and whispered, "you gotta be good or the preacher will whip you after church!"

I goggled at her. She had pretty, light brown hair, tucked into two braids, and slightly buck teeth. She was wearing a subdued plaid dress that came down to the middle of her knees and made her look like she belonged in that 'farmer and his wife' painting that you see all over the place. But her

87

eyes were friendly, and I liked her smile.

I whispered back, "Only if I don't whip him first!"

The teacher turned around, and just like that, the girl's face went as blank as a sheet of new paper. Now I was really creeped out. We spent forty-five minutes listening to the teacher lecture us about how children who are not baptized will go to Hell and burn forever. No crayons, no cute pictures of Jesus surrounded by fluffy sheep, No cookies or crackers or anything. Just blah, blah, blah non-stop until I thought my ears were gonna bleed.

But that wasn't the worst of it. After Sunday School, we all trooped upstairs for a bunch of sitting, standing, singing and praying, and then the pastor got up there and started yacking away.

"I know it says in your programs that the sermon today is going to be *Preparing for the Apocalypse*, but we're going to talk about something else today. A young child walked up to me this morning, right on the very steps of our church. And she was dressed like a *Wanton*! With skirts above her knees, and lipstick on her lips and her hair all hanging down loose like some heathen from New York!"

He stopped and glared right at me, his face turning red, and a number of other folks turned to look at me, too. I know my mouth hung open, because I could feel myself gaping at him.

"And when I attempted to help this young lady, out of the goodness of my Christian Soul, she mocked me with her smart little mouth, and told me that she does not even know where her parents are. Her own parents have abandoned her to her sin, and she wallows in the pridefulness of her evil ways! Then she forced her way into our church!"

I started eyeballing the exits. This was not good, but I was in the

88

middle of the pew, and would have to climb over half-a-dozen people to escape. I decided to hold my ground unless they started physically coming after me.

"Little does she know of the wrath of God toward misbehaving children – children who are not mild-mannered, obedient, and respectful of their elders. She does not know that when the children mocked Elisha, prophet of God, that bears were sent to tear them apart – forty-two children dead because they disrespected the servant of the Lord!"

I saw the girl from Sunday school a couple of rows up. She seemed to be the only one who wasn't staring at me. Her hands were folded and she was gazing down at them miserably. I felt a stir of pity for her that she had been listening to this shit day after day for who knows how long.

"Happy shall the parent be that takes the disobedient child and dasheth him upon the stones!" There was a swelling chorus of amens from all around me. Jesus, these people were all crazy.

I shot up from my seat, not realizing what I was doing until I was already standing. The pastor's fat red face was dripping with sweat as he pointed a finger at me.

"Behold! I reveal this Jezebel to you, that you may know her and shun her!"

I stood on the seat and pointed back. "Fuck you, you nasty old son-of-a-bitch. I wouldn't listen to you if the road to heaven was an escalator and you were working the on/off button!"

There was a muffled snort in the dead silence that followed my speech, and I tried not to look at the Sunday school girl, pretty sure that it was her, trying to cover a laugh. I hopped up on the back of the pew and

89

made my escape leaping over the heads of the people seated between me and the door. A few folks made half-hearted grabs, but most of them just seemed plain old shocked. As I reached the safety of the floor, the preacher hollered after me, "Someday, you'll beg for our help, you spawn of Satan! You'll be burning in the pit, writhing in torment and beg for the sweet, cool water of salvation. And it shall be denied you!"

I turned around for one last, parting shot. "And if you were burning in the pit of Hell, you dumb fuck, I wouldn't piss on your teeth to put out the fire in your mouth!" Then I ran like hell all the way home.

Needless to say, I didn't go back.

Now

Chapter Eleven: Of Rainbows and Llamas

The first thing I noticed about Rock Head was that it was really, really small. And that it was really, really full of people. The people seemed mostly to belong to one of two groups; first, there were the citizeny, touristy mainstreamers, complete with expensive clothes, cameras and goofy hats.

Then there was an entirely other type of group of people, who all looked like they were related in some intimate, tribal way to Lake and Willow. Dusty, young, and weird. They had as many piercings, tattoos and fetishes as the other guys had credit cards. Most amazing of all, everyone appeared to be mixing and mingling with equanimity. They even looked like they were having fun. Cantaloupes flaunted themselves everywhere, a fleshy, succulent spectacle.

Lake had stood up again, and was waving and yelling at people he recognized in the crowd. Willow directed me through the mob and down Main Street to an auto repair shop.

Banners announcing the 35th Annual Rock Head Cantaloupe Festival were draped across every available space. We passed a fair set up around the town green, surrounding a really, really obvious phallic symbol masquerading as a ten-foot obelisk with the town's name painted on it. The fair was complete with all the corn-pone components thereof, including a calliope, a Ferris wheel, and a penny arcade. From my seat high in the van, I could see what looked like a melon-eating contest going on. Visions of vodka-soaked fruit danced in my head.

I hoped the liquor store was open.

*

The guy at the auto shop was falling under the spell of the Cantaloupe Festival, but managed to pull himself back into this dimension long enough to look at the radiator in the Roadster and pronounce it fixable without needing parts – right away. "Yeah," he said, foot tapping to the beat of a band set up in the park. "It's cracked all right, but I can jimmy it up to last you to LA. You'll be able to find a new radiator there, no problem."

He was already looking out the big front window of the shop again. I had to wave my hand in front of his face to get his attention.

"Hey, Cantaloupe Master. When can you have it fixed by?"

"Huh?"

I repeated the question, and refrained from kicking him in the nuts to jog his brain. Behind him, Willow smothered a giggle. Must have been the look on my face.

"Oh, I reckon I could get it done for you by tomorrow morning. That suit you okay?"

I relaxed. A little. More than one day in this corn pone – I mean cantaloupe-pone – town, and brain cells were going to start jumping out my ears and leaping to their little deaths. But one night, I could handle.

I laid a fifty on him and we walked back outside where Lake was busy chatting up a couple of guys that could have been blood relatives. If, of course, his blood relatives were traditionally dressed Russian peasants with dreadlocks and multiple face piercings. Between the two of them, I counted at least a dozen – face piercings, not dreadlocks. God only knew what else they had pierced that was hidden by those goofy Cossack pants.

"Hey," said Lake when we emerged. "Car gonna be okay? I fell in

92

love just riding in it. Man, was it cool." He turned back to the two guys he had been yacking with. "Classic convertible, dudes. Leather interior, fold-back rag-top. Pristine."

The other two glanced at me and Grandma Rose with interest, then at Willow. "We're having an Aymara Ceremony tonight. Lusia is here."

Willow sparked with excitement and laid a hand on my arm. "It's very good karma to participate in one of Lusia's ceremonies. Will you go with us?"

Before I could answer, Grandma Rose piped up for both of us. "A real Aymara ceremony? With a llama and everything? I've always wanted to see one of those. We'll be there. Just let us drop our stuff off at the hotel. We'll meet you back in the square?"

I looked at her in amazement. "What the hell is an Aymara ceremony, and why do you know about them when I don't? And what the fuck do they do with the llama?"

Grandma Rose grinned. "You ought to stay home and watch the Discovery Channel once in a while, smarty pants." With that, she set off in search of a likely hotel. I made a face at Willow, who was laughing again, and took off after Grandma.

*

"The Aymara are a people that live in the Andes," Grandma explained over dinner. "They worship the Goddess Pachamana."

Willow added, "Tonight, Lusia will be holding a thanksgiving ceremony to Pachamana for all her blessings. By participating, we will be lending our support to a tradition of nature worship that goes back a thousand years."

93

"Oh, great," I said. "That sounds even more exciting than the melon-ballers contest." No one seemed to notice I was being sarcastic.

*

The ceremony actually started at midnight, and was held in a big field about a mile from downtown Rock Head. It was led by a gorgeous dark-skinned woman with long, dark hair, and a pale blue jumpsuit of some flimsy material that clung to her like a coat of butter. The bonfires were built and waiting, and as she took a long torch and lit the piles of log and lumber that were scattered through our space, she called out in a loud, clear voice, "My name is Lusia Parizien, and my Momma was a Voodoo Queen, and my Daddy was a Brujo from Bolivia."

She finished lighting the last bonfire, and stood to face the excited crowd, torch held aloft. "Now, I take all the knowledge and craft of the voodoo peoples, and all the piety and wisdom of the Aymara, and I put them to the use of the Rainbow People!"

She gestured with a hand, and all four fires flared up in bright colored flames that made it look for a moment as if we were indeed inside a rainbow. Cheers erupted everywhere.

"Tonight, we join together to honor the Goddess of the Moon and of the Sun, and the God of the Earth. Tonight, we will dance and sing and pray together, and ask that their blessings be bestowed upon us and our poisoned Earth – to make ourselves whole, and our planet as well. We are the Rainbow People – the last free Peoples of the Americas!" More cheering. It could have been boring, but the woman herself was so charismatic that it was hard not to revel in her every gesture. Her voice was throaty and compelling.

She danced with the torch held high, through the crowd, and

94

shouted out, "We refuse to live by the rules of others. We're the Gypsies of freedom; we go wherever the Goddess wills us!"

Someone took up a drum, then a couple more people started banging on whatever was handy, and before I knew it, we were part of a big snake dance that wound around the clearing and the bonfires and back on its own tail. We danced in long lines and big circles that looked like a Bolivian version of the Hokey Pokey, while the Bruja in blue sang song after song in Creole and in what I assumed was Aymarian, bellowed back to her by all us dancers at the top of our lungs.

The sounds of fists and sticks on drums, on thighs, on trees, threaded a steady, seductive beat that enveloped everything. The belting was lubricated by jugs full of singani, a type of Bolivian grape brandy that Lake assured me was a paint-searing 90 proof.

Good enough for me, I could hokey pokey and bellow drunkenly with the best of them. It wasn't rock and roll, for sure, but there was a sparky leap of camaraderie that reminded me of a rock concert, as goofy as that sounds. When you're holding hands with five hundred people, and dancing your ass off around a bonfire, loaded on Brazilian Goo-Goo Juice and being urged on by the most beautiful woman you've ever seen, a wild sense of anything-is-okay togetherness swamps hang-ups and suspicion and common sense.

Just before dawn, the dancing stopped, and silence rushed in to fill the void left by brandied throats. Lusia stood in front of the hushed, expectant crowd.

Grandma Rose stood on her tippy-toes to watch, until a couple of good-natured Willowites decided to lift her onto their shoulders so she could

95

see.

Lusia motioned for a large wooden box to be brought to her. She opened it and took out a blanket, which unfolded into a beautiful, brightly colored woven cloth which she set on the ground in front of her. A derby, turned up for donations, came next. She carefully unwound the wrappings from a long, wooden staff carved with lightening symbols, and laid it reverently on the cloth, then took a series of big seashells and laid them in a curved pattern across the blanket, followed by three plates that went in front. "The staff represents lightening, the Holy Masculine and the land," whispered Lake. "The seashells are for the Holy Feminine, the Sun and the Moon," he continued.

The shells were filled with carnations and incense, then money and candy, dried fern and sugar, and finally with candied figurines. The plates were filled with colorful scraps of cotton, meat, small potatoes and barley. Then they were sprinkled with more singani. The whole while, Lusia was chanting and singing, occasionally looking up and exhorting the heavens as she wove gracefully back and forth in front of the blanket.

Finally, just as dawn was breaking, Lusia reached into the box for the final item. "What the hell is that?" I said, to no one in particular. "It looks like a fucking Muppet on a stick."

"Sacrifice. Mummified llama fetus," said one of the guys holding Grandma Rose aloft.

"No shit?" I said, and forced my way through the crowd to get a better look. Sure enough, the tall, skinny Muppet with an alligator skull tacked on turned out to be a desiccated baby llama corpse. Huge, hollow eye-sockets rode above the sharp jaws, and the legs were tied together around the pole it topped.

Lusia took it and held it high, chanting loudly, then passed it to one of the dancers standing near her, who then passed it on to someone else. As the mummified llama fetus made the rounds, Lusia sang several more prayers in a language that creaked with age. Power crackled in the air, along with sparks from the fires. When Lusia took the llama back, she moved swiftly to tie up the shell and plate offerings in bright cotton bags. Then she secured the contents of the plates to the lightening staff and the shells to the llama. The incessantly beating drums stopped, and in complete silence, she said one final word – "Pachamana!" – and everybody screamed it after her as she threw the staff and the fetus on the fire, just as dawn broke. Just like before, all four bonfires flared up in a rainbow blaze. A fragrant, fruity, meaty smell filled the air.

Bedlam broke out, people hollering and laughing, scarves and hats being thrown in the air, singani being poured over peoples' heads and down their throats, and drums going wild.

Holding a gigantic seashell full of grape brandy in her hands, black derby materializing on her head, Lusia moved through the crowd, laughing and bestowing blessings. The closer she got, the more beautiful I realized she was.

Finally, she got to me and Grandma, who was set back on her own feet for our meeting. Lusia dipped a finger in the singani, and dotted it on Grandma Rose's forehead. "There's a man waiting for you, hoping you will choose him for your husband," Lusia said.

"Hot damn," replied Grandma Rose. "You sure about that?"

Lusia laughed and winked at me. "Hot damn, I am. He's been waiting

97

to meet you for a while, sexy one. Don't make him wait too much longer. He's not getting any younger."

She moved to me, dipped a finger in the brandy and pressed her wet finger to my forehead. "You, on the other hand, have several men waiting for you. Your life has changed, and it's about to change even more. Have fun!"

"You sure it's gonna be fun?" I asked, thinking sourly about the changes that had happened so far.

She burst into laughter. "Ladies and Gentlemen, take my advice! Pull down your pants, and slide on the ice!"

I blinked at her. Hey, where had that come from? Then I remembered and I reached out to catch her and ask her how the hell she knew about that, but she had already moved beyond me to another waiting couple.

I was exhausted, although Rosie-O looked like she could go another polka or two. Old people. They never know when to quit. Willow and Lake agreed to see her safely home, so I went back to our hotel room to crash. Before I hit the sheets, I powered up my laptop and checked my messages. Sure enough, there was one from Max. There were a few others, too, but I deleted the rest unread.

I've been thinking about what you wrote about how happy the people you met in Kansas were, Max wrote. *They sound really brave at the heart of it. Brave enough to be who they are, do what is right for them. I don't know if I've got that kind of courage, myself. Sure, I live a little outside the box, but not that much. I wonder who I would be if I just let myself be. Scary thought. You?*

I lay on my back, laptop on my chest, screen tilted so I could read it, and thought about what Max had said. Was that really what this was all about? Bravery? Fear? After a couple of minutes, I wrote him back. *Until I got fired, I thought I knew exactly who I was. And I did think I was a very brave person. Ten feet tall and bullet-proof. Now I'm not so sure, because I've been terrified just about every day about what I'm supposed to do next. Maybe I don't know myself as well as I thought I did. Oh, well. I think I'll sleep on it for a while. Nite, Eve.*

99

Then

Chapter Twelve: In-Out, Good-Bad, Done

There aren't many things I really regret – really regret, not 'shouldn't have had that last potato chip' regret. I'm not sure I regret this one either, but it was one of those train wreck kind of things that I knew was going to fuck me up no matter what, and I let it happen anyway.

It happened about ten years ago, and started when I got a call from the producers of the Annual Galveston Music Festival. The GMF was a huge awards event that covered the entire island, from the Aztec Bar to the Zydeco Dome. Bands came from all over the United States and Europe to participate, and gave some of the finest live performances I'd ever seen. I was invited to fly out on their dime and participate in various ceremonies and hosting duties on behalf of the twenty or so Detroit bands that were gonna be there.

I was kind of waffling about whether or not to go, until I realized that I had been asked over the music editor, and he was fuming. Can't help that I'm popular, now, can I? I ended up accepting just to piss him off.

Then I found out that Blue was going, too. It just seemed friendly to fly out together and hang out a little. Christ, we saw each other every day.

We had hooked up for breakfast in this little dive restaurant down the street from the hotel, and were eating black beans and salsa over scrambled eggs, washed down by Rolling Rock, and laughing our asses off. We didn't have anything to do the first day except enjoy, so we decided to slide off down to the beach.

Blue called and reserved a cabana to change clothes in, and then we walked downtown until we found a shop with hot swim wear. He grabbed a

100

pair of baggy, neon blue trunks, while I went for a basic black bikini.

We reached the cabana and changed clothes modestly beside the separate screens set up for that purpose, then hit the beach. The sun and sand were hot, the water was salty and cold. We ran in and out, body surfing and teeth chattering and lips turning blue, then warming up in the sun until our skin pinked, like true mid-westerners. It was corny, but it was cracking me up, and Blue had picked up a twelve of Dos Equis on the way over, which we were icing in the tiny cabana sink, so that was okay, too.

I was shivering with cold when I finally called uncle and lay down on a blanket in the hot sun to thaw out. Blue joined me, still winded from his last attempt at body surfing.

There was a stream of warm sand on my belly, and I squinted my eyes open to see that it was falling from Blue's open palm.

"I could bury you in sand," he offered. "That's something people do at beaches."

I shaded my eyes with my hands to see if he was serious, and then got caught in a strange look in his eyes. It occurred to me that he was thinking about kissing me, and I shrugged just enough to make my bikini move. He leaned over me, really, really slowly, and kept his eyes on mine as he blistered my lips with his.

He stayed close, leaning in, and licked his lips, then reached down and licked mine.

I was hot and cold and all mixed up, and before I could figure it out, he surged over my body with a power that left me breathless.

He tasted of salsa and beer and smelled of ocean, and when he linked our fingers and pillowed our joined hands under my head, something

101

surged inside of me, too. He slid a leg between mine, and bumped our feet together. Then he pulled back to grin at me like a teenager. Pure joy, pure friendship, pure delight. He let go of my hands to run his up and down my body, sweeping away the sand he had rained down on me a few minutes earlier.

"You're my hero, you know that? How did you get to be so strong and so fragile at the same time?"

I fisted my fingers in his hair to tether him to me. Just for a little while, just my secret need to have someone strong enough to hang onto.

He kissed me again, and then rested his forehead on mine as he said, "I want to make love with you, I want to be inside you, I want to make you need me. Go back to the hotel with me, and we can lay around and have room service and fuck until our ears bleed."

I wasn't sure if I could let go long enough to walk sedately back to the hotel. I was wrapped around him like a drowning woman who's found a life preserver under her fingers just as she's about to go down for the last time.

I was desperate to stay linked with him without letting him know how crippled I felt, how much I was afraid that if we separated our twined bodies to walk back to the hotel, that painful, pure lust would disappear and he'd just be Blue again, and I'd just be one of those creepy groupie women who bang the boss for a paycheck.

He must have caught the whirl of my thoughts, because he brushed his lips across mine and said, "or, we could take a shower and go to the cabana for a while?" He raised an eyebrow at me.

"I am really sandy," I said. "I have sand in places. . ."

102

". . . that I would be delighted to make sand-free for you," he finished, and scooped me up into his arms and carried me to the series of fresh water showers that ranged in front of the little beach houses. After we were clean, we joined hands and dashed for the cabana.

It was tiny, about ten by ten, with a cot and a small table. It was about ten thousand degrees and there was a sink in one corner, which was currently cooling our beer.

Blue stepped away and out of his trunks, waiting patiently while I looked at him. He was really, really beautiful, in a way that made my throat clench. He looked happy and relaxed as he stood there, waiting for me. He also had a hard-on roughly the size of Liberty's Torch, which wasn't a penlight, by any means.

I took off my own suit and stood for a minute, letting him look as well. Then we moved toward each other, and he stroked me, breasts, belly, thighs, with feather-light hands until I shuddered and stepped closer, pulling his head down so I could get his mouth back on mine.

He moved with a shattering strength and urgency that took me by surprise, placing his hands on my ass and picking me up off my feet to plunge inside me. I lost my breath. For a moment, the air backed up in my lungs, and I couldn't remember how to push it in and out. My heart paused in the middle of a beat. There was a snick in my head. "The key's in the lock," I thought, wildly. Everything was different.

He buried his face in my hair and started to move inside of me. Every thrust went straight to my heart, and I licked sweat and shower water from his neck, shaking with the knowledge that this man was in me.

He shifted to capture my mouth with his again, thrusting harder and

103

faster. He wrenched his mouth away, and I fisted his hair, trying to pull him back. He stopped moving to laugh out a shaky breath and reached up to brush a strand of wet hair from my forehead. He put his forehead on mine as he gulped air, and said, "Do you need more time, Babe? I'm going to come inside you, and I want you ready. I'm not going to stop, I'm not going to pull out or pull away or wait for you or be controlled or gentle or any of those other sensitive-new-age guy things. I feel like a fucking animal."

He was rubbing against me as he spoke, and my head was swimming with lust and power. I was soaked with sweat and weightless with desire. I was slick with my own juice and I could feel it hot as lava on my thighs. I clenched around him, hard, and he roared against my mouth.

He made a spectacular thrust and I could feel him pulsing inside me as he buried his face in my hair and said my name like a mantra. My own orgasm burst on me like a sunrise, and I jerked against him and moaned in my throat as tears leaked down my checks and I couldn't figure out why.

I thought we were done, until Blue carried me over and laid me down on the cot, sliding in next to me to explore my entire body with those amazing hands, until I came again and wept from the pleasure and the tenderness of it while he held me in steady arms and brushed the tears away with his lips.

We spooned up, and I tried to figure out what the hell had happened, but I was exhausted from the best sex of my life and the attempt to dog paddle through the messy sea of what normal people probably felt all the time. The last thing I remembered for a couple of hours was the sound of Blue's breath slowing in sleep.

*

When I woke up, the air had cooled down, and it was getting chilly, except for the places that we were pressed together.

Blue stretched and tightened his arms around me. "Eve, you awake?"

I had no idea in the world how we were supposed to get out of there, so I relaxed back against him and waited for a clue. He ran scalding lips across my shoulder and up my neck. "You feeling okay, beautiful? I really was an animal."

"Jesus, Blue, I'm a woman, not a bowl of whipped cream," I said. I swung my feet over the side of the cot as he started laughing.

"Okay, then I guess it'll be okay to let my inner animal go nuts." I started to stand up, when he snaked out and grabbed me. Swinging himself around on the bed, he planted his teeth on my ass and bit me. A fuse started sparking in my clit, and traveled north and south until my brain sizzled and my toes curled.

"Turnabout is fair play. Come bite me back, pretty lady."

I considered him, naked and waiting for me, arms open. It was tempting, but I was starving. "Can't. I'm too hungry. If I bite you now, I might not let loose."

"Easy enough to fix," Blue said, reaching for his cell phone. While I got dressed, he called and asked for steak and champagne to be sent up to his hotel room, then put on his own clothes, whistling. We walked back to the hotel barefoot and holding hands. I felt like I was about twelve. And I liked it.

We ate and fucked and went for a swim and fucked some more and hopped in the jacuzzi and drank champagne and fucked again, and a crazy part of my brain was wondering if this really was making love. Maybe. I'd never tried that before.

We had sex on the bed, sex on the balcony, sex on the floor. We were lying side by side when he grabbed me and placed me on top of him, linking our hands and stretching them out over his head so my nipples bobbed in his face like ripe grapes. I could feel his hard-on growing against me.

He looked up at me and smiled. "Eve, show me what it's like to put myself in your hands." So I did. I was rough and careless and used teeth and nails and tongue, howling my pleasure to show how much I craved him.

When we were both ready to orgasm, he grabbed my hips and plunged deep. Then we were both animals, and when we came I stopped worrying about how to leave.

I collapsed on top of him and he wrapped his arms around me and whispered in my ear, "I love you, Eve. Have ever since the first time I saw you. Are you ready to love me back?"

His breathing evened out and he fell asleep and I still hadn't answered his question. He thought he knew me, but he had no idea what he was asking me for. Blue was so . . . unbroken by life. I couldn't begin to fathom the amount of pain I would feel if I let him take that little fissure he had carved out in my heart, and allow him to finish breaking it away so he could come inside.

I just couldn't do it. Couldn't even consider it. What was wrong with me was not fixable with true love's kiss. I leaned over in the dark and whispered into his ear as he slept. "I love you, too, Blue. But I'll never be ready." Then I slipped on my clothes and split.

*

The next morning, a pounding on my door woke me up. Blue didn't look particularly pissed off or injured or anything, but his steady gaze still made me wince.

"You left. I'm not a coward, or an idiot. We should talk."

Somehow, I didn't think I would have much luck getting dressed with him in the room, without jumping him bodily and ripping his pants off with my teeth. "I'll meet you in the hotel restaurant in half an hour." With each word, I watched his eyes go cooler.

"Of course. I'll meet you there."

*

In the hotel restaurant, I pushed food I didn't want around on my plate, and tried to be flip instead of miserable. "Look, Blue, I like you a lot – we've been friends for a long time. But I'm not ready for all this commitment jazz just because of one hot weekend away from home. I'm never gonna be ready for all this commitment shit. What you're looking for is some hip blond who looks good in pastels and knows when to keep her mouth shut."

He leaned back in his chair and looked at me disbelievingly. "If you really believe that shit, you're crazy."

"Yeah, I get told that a lot," I said, acid on my tongue.

His hand shot out and captured mine, and he rubbed a thumb over the pulse in my wrist, which immediately shot up to about Mach five. Christ!

I pulled my hand away. "Fuckin' A, Blue. We're friends, we work together. We went out of town and had a friendly weekend fuck party. Don't push me."

He raised an eyebrow and almost smiled, and I knew I wasn't fooling him at all.

"Peace. Maybe you're right, Eve. And it doesn't matter what the

107

reason is, or what you say it is. If we're both not there, it's not happening. I'm sorry I pushed, Eve. But you've got this protective bubble around you, and it keeps a lot of good things out."

"Maybe," I answered. "But if I do, it's my bubble, and my choice."

Blue shook his head. "Yeah. But that bubble isn't reality, Eve. Someday you're going to crash head into it. And it's gonna hurt like hell."

I was having a little trouble following that one. "Crash into what?"

"What else? The *real.*"

He stood up and raised my hand to his lips, then pressed a kiss on my open palm. Then he folded my fingers closed as if to guard the kiss he had placed there. "Keep that for when you need it, darling."

Then he left. We never talked about it again.

Now

Chapter Thirteen: Of Wild Men and Pocket Protectors

We had breakfast with Lake and Willow before heading out of town. They planned on joining a caravan of other Rainbow People and heading out to California to sign on as seasonal labor at a vineyard – shades of Cesar Chavez.

"There's one thing I never found out," said Willow, as we were saying our goodbyes. "Who's Steven Tyler?"

"Geez, Willow," said Lake, before I could answer. "Even I know that. He was the drummer for Cream."

It was one of the few times in my life I had been startled speechless.

*

We decided to nurse the Roadster along carefully until we were sure the radiator braise was going to hold, so when we got as far as Paradox, Colorado, we stopped for the night, and stayed in the red rocks in a Mexican Hacienda-style bed and breakfast that offered peace and quiet, sans Rainbow People, murderous jugglers or incestuous perverts. Boring, in other words, but it let me catch up on my sleep.

Grandma Rose had wandered down to the kitchen to watch our hostess make tamales, so I took the opportunity to power up my laptop and check my messages. There was a long one from Max, and a shorter one from Blue which I deleted unread. The more time went by, the more angry I got with him. He sold my fucking magazine, for Christ's sake, and I didn't really have anything to say to him, besides "fuck you, too."

Max's message started off with the usual stuff about the gallery and

109

Freddie. *I tried painting this morning, partly because it scares me, and we were talking about fear and courage. I do a lot of things that people think are brave, but putting what's inside me out there for people to opinionate all over? That's really scary. I'll show you what I'm working on when I see you again, if you like. Blue stopped by. Have you talked to him yet?*

I was glad to hear that Max was painting again; I thought he was much better than he did, but what the hell was up with him and Blue becoming buddies all of a sudden?

I checked it out, and sure enough, even though nobody from Aerosmith lives anywhere remotely near Los Angeles, they're all going to be there for a week, as of Tuesday. Promoting a game, believe it or not. You are really scary sometimes, darling. And I mean that in the most admiring way possible. But are you scared?

He went on, asking me about Grandma Rose and what was happening on the road and when I thought we'd be in LA. I spent a fun half hour writing back to regale him with tales of the Rainbow People and the Bolivian Bruja, then smoked a quiet joint with Grandma Rose. It was hard to enjoy, because I was swamped with the thought that I was getting high not for fun, but to leash the fear that crawled around inside me. Finally, the blessed THC kicked in and I gave it all up to eat some smokin' tamales given to us by the lady that ran the place. Belly full, tired and stoned, I finally crashed out.

*

The next morning we got up relatively early, pigged out on crepes and homemade muffins, and hit the road. Our destination was Bryce Canyon, another one of Grandma Rose's Discovery Channel locations, and we reached

110

there late afternoon.

Looking at Bryce Canyon is like looking at the ocean. I felt like what was happening with me was so small compared to this, that it hardly mattered at all. Like I could just wander off and start another small life somewhere, and everything would just be alright. We hit Ruby's Inn, which not only had a huge place at the entrance of the Park, but also made cabin rentals at the top of the Canyon. We grabbed some groceries from Ruby's store and a place of our own. "There's only three other cabins up there being used right now," said the cashier as she handed us our key. "Bunch of business guys are on a retreat, doing some kind of seminar in two of the cabins, and the facilitator is in a third one."

"Sweet," I replied. Another night like we had in Paradox, and I'd be ready for LA.

As we headed up the twisty road toward our cabin, the air cooled off and began to smell amazingly wonderful. I've spent a lot of time in the city; I'd forgotten that pine air freshener was actually based on a real smell that was about a thousand times better.

The road ended in a parking area that you could see the canyon from. We hopped out of the car and walked to the edge, and the world reached out and totally amazed me.

Bryce Canyon isn't just a big hole in the dirt. From where we were standing, it was an endless parade of what Grandma Rose called hoodoos – towers of rock that had been carved by water and time, some of them no wider than the roadster, but stretching up to the sky hundreds of feet from their roots in the canyon floor.

"I'm having a hard time remembering exactly why I think

111

everything in the universe isn't ticking away just fine, whether I know it or not," said Rosie-O.

I don't know how long I stood there, holding hands with her and gawking like a kid, not thinking at all. My brain was as empty as a sieve. Until some loudmouthed blockhead came howling up the hiking path below us, and pulled me right out of my reverie.

"Could you kindly shut the fuck up?" I said. "I'm trying to have a moment here."

My voice startled him, and he lost his footing. He scrambled to regain his balance, coming perilously close to the cliff-edge of the trail he was hiking. Grandma Rose and I raced to catch hold of him and pull him to safety before he went over the side.

We got a good grip on him and pulled him bodily off the trail and up into the clearing, then sat him on a rock. He looked like he was going to cry. While I was waiting for him to decide whether or not he was going to go into cardiac arrest, I had the time to actually look at him.

The guy was in the middle of a national park, actually hiking a trail in a national park, and he was wearing a white shirt, a really boring tie, and slacks and loafers. Just to make sure no one mistook what kind of guy he was, he'd finished off his look with glasses that had heavy black frames, and short hair slicked back with some shiny junk that looked suspiciously like Brylcreem.

Christ, he was probably wearing Hai Karate, too, but I wasn't going to get close enough again to confirm that theory.

Grandma Rose eyed him curiously. "Is that a pocket protector?"

He shifted defensively. "Maybe. Why?"

"Well, I was wondering what the hell is up here that your pocket needs protecting from."

"Chipmunks," he said, eyes sweeping the clearing as if he expected an onslaught of the little bastards momentarily. "I keep my nuts in there."

"Well, that's one place to keep 'em that I never heard of before," I said, but before he could ask me what I meant, half-a-dozen similarly clad men came straggling up the path and joined us.

Bringing up the rear was a lithe blond guy with a soul patch and a lime-green, loosely woven cotton shirt and jeans. He was the only one in the bunch wearing hiking boots.

All of the white shirts had taken seats primly on the boulders dotting the clearing. Green shirt sauntered over, smiling, hands in pockets and introduced himself. "Hi. I'm Antlers Puck. And no, I have no explanation for that. Don't even bother asking," he said, when Rosie-O opened her mouth. "What's going on? Dicker okay?" With a nod of his head he indicated Mr. Pocket Protector.

"Hello," replied Rosie-O. "I'm Rose, and this is my granddaughter, Eve. We're on our way to Los Angeles to meet with Steven Tyler, the rock star. Eve needs to talk to him, but I just want to--"

"Your friend is fine," I said quickly. I had more than a suspicion of where Grandma Rose was heading with *that* one. "He stumbled right at the top, and lost his balance. We just helped him get back on his feet."

Puck sighed and gave Dicker a dark look. "Story of his life. Almost all the way to the top, then he screws up and someone else has to rescue him."

"What do you mean?"

He sighed again. "Look at him. Richard 'Dick' Dicker. All those other

113

guys work for him." They were all clustered around him now, listening to his story and clucking in sympathy. Water bottles and handkerchiefs were offered, one guy was actually fanning him. They made a tableau of solicitude in failure. "He's spearheading his company's hostile takeover of a competitor. He was supposed to be performing a leadership exercise by leading his men on a hike that my great-great-grandmother couldn't have fucked up."

Now I was curious. "What do you have to do with all this? You don't look like you're in the same galaxy, much less company."

Again with the dark look. "I do personal and corporate growth seminars for top-line male management who feel they've lost touch with their inner, intuitive wild man. We're here having a Wild Man Weekend."

I looked at the other guys. "What the hell kind of company do they run?"

Puck sighed again. "Pocket protector manufacturing and supply. They're taking over another pocket protector company."

I started snickering. I couldn't stop myself.

Puck sighed again. He sure did that a lot. "I don't suppose either of you ladies would happen to have a joint on you?"

*

Puck gave his merry men an hour off to shower and regroup, and helped us stow our bags and groceries in our cabin. When we were done, we smoked another joint out of Frank's pot stash.

We talked in a desultory fashion about masculine power, emotional commitment and getting in touch with your inner animal. Some of it sounded like fun, and when Puck invited us to join them for dinner and a campfire circle, we accepted with pleasure.

"I've always wanted to get in touch with my inner animal," said Grandma Rose. "But what if my inner animal isn't very assertive? Like if it's a panda or a sloth or something?"

"Sloths can get pretty mean," said Puck, kicked back on the couch. "And pandas will rip your head off if you get in between them and their eucalyptus leaves."

"That's koala bears," I said.

"What is?"

"It's koala bears that eat eucalyptus leaves. Panda bears eat bamboo shoots."

"Gotcha," said Puck. "Bamboo shoots, then. It's all a matter of priorities. Even a panda will get you if you come between them and their bamboo shoots. Rip your head off." He looked at me. "Right?"

"Right."

"Well, good, then," said Grandma Rose. "Tonight, I'm gonna let my inner panda go nuts."

I couldn't wait to see this one.

*

Dinner was sizzling away on a big, open-air grill, although I wasn't sure how many of the 'wild men' were planning on chowing down, since dinner centered around some big, juicy steaks. Turns out most of them were more chicken or fish guys. Puck managed to come up with some chicken breast fillets, and the gang settled down; it was the closest they'd come to assertive since we'd hauled Dicker's clumsy ass away from the cliff.

"Okay," said Puck when the guys had finished chomping on chicken and were working on a Boston creme pie for dessert. "Now, we're going to

115

pass around the sacred chalice, and practice visualization."

Grandma Rose leaned over to me and whispered, "I thought the sacred chalice was a symbol of the sacred vagina, didn't you?"

Puck sailed blithely forward. "As you drink, I want you to form a picture of your fully realized masculine self, and--"

"Mr. Puck?" interrupted Dicker.

Sigh. "Yes?"

"You mean we're all going to drink out of the same glass? Because I have a weak immune system, and . . ."

"Maybe everyone could pour a small amount into their own individual cups from the sacred chalice," said another guy. Puck fixed him with a look of disbelief.

"After all, we wouldn't want employees to get sick because of an unhygienic ritual, now, would we?" Dicker interjected self-righteously. There was a subdued chorus of approval for Dicker's caution.

"Oh, Jesus," I muttered, and stood up, grabbing the wine goblet out of Puck's hand. I held it up in a toast, and shouted loud enough for my voice to echo wildly in the canyon, "Ladies and Gentlemen, take my advice; pull down your pants and slide on the ice!" I looked them all in the eye, then took a healthy swig and handed it off to the guy sitting next to me. "Go ahead, I dare you!"

He looked doubtfully at me, and then at the goblet, while everyone waited.

Just when I had given up seeing anything happen at all, he said, "what the Hell!" and lifted the decorative cup to his lips and took a careful sip. Then he passed it over with a challenging look.

"Bootstraps and bull balls!" said the next guy, rising to his feet.

And so it went. When it got around to Grandma Rose, she leapt to her feet and hollered. "May you all have enough challenges to keep life from ever being boring!" Then she killed off the rest and threw the goblet in the fire. Unfortunately, it was plastic, so it stunk up the clearing for a few minutes, but hey.

The group warmed up significantly; Puck was hopping around, getting everybody to make growling noises and visualize their inner animal, which was really weird, considering that most of these guys didn't look like they had an inner goldfish. It was starting to be almost fun. Well, maybe not almost fun, but almost tolerable. Until Puck pulled me aside and whispered, "I'm not sure your Grandma should have drunk any of that."

"Why not?"

"I spiked it to get these guys moving."

"What the hell did you spike it with?"

"LSD?" he said, apologetically.

"You put LSD in the wine and then let my grandmother drink it? Puck, you are such an asshole." I stared at him for a moment, but he had gotten distracted and was looking back at some idiot running around making horns with his fingers and head-butting everybody. Puck's face was shiny in the firelight, and I realized he'd imbibed a little, too.

"Puck? Puck!" He turned around, and I slugged him in the jaw hard enough to whip him 180 degrees before he collapsed on the ground.

The wild men cheered. Wildly.

*

Once Puck was out of commission, we decided to move the party indoors and play strip poker. I grabbed a fifth and we did shooters, while Dicker tried to get my clothes off, and Grandma tried to get her clothes off. Fortunately for everybody, we were all wearing quite a bit of stuff – Dicker had two pocket protectors and garters holding his socks up, for Christ's sake – and nobody ended up very naked.

I went out to check on the guys who had been delegated to put the fire out, and was captured by the beauty of the stars and the quarter moon. The dark was a lively place that night, and I slipped down onto the ground to lean my back against a rock, watching as our two temporary firemen would pour a little bit of water on the campfire, and then *ohh* and *ahh* over the streaking smoke and spark. The acid did make it look amazing, nearly as amazing as the dancing stars and the trails of visible air that blew across my face.

I closed my eyes and leaned my head back. Even with my eyes closed, I could see the stars dancing. Then a cooler wind started blowing, and a heavy cloud scudded in. A deep voice boomed out of it, and I realized I was no longer sitting on the ground, covered in black leather. Instead, I was standing on a mountain, with the canyon at my feet. I was dressed in coarsely woven brown cloth, a long robe of some kind, and clutching two stone tablets in my hands.

"Stop lying around and get your shit together, for Christ's sake," boomed the big voice.

"I'm having some real problems here," I argued. "Cut me some fuckin' slack!"

There was a pause, then God said, "No slack! Did Moses ask for slack? David? No, damn it, they went out there and got their shit together

118

and did what they were damn well told. Moses had a stutter, did you know that? Turned him into one of the best damn orators you could find anywhere."

"Yeah, but was he happy?"

"Well," God hedged.

Before he could say any more, another big cloud scudded up, a mouth I'd know anywhere grinning down at me. The lips pursed and blew the God cloud away.

Then they turned to me. "You're not doing so bad, kid. He's just a little cranky. He's old. Problems with his kid. Old man wants him to be a carpenter, son wants to be a cultural icon . . . you know how it goes."

"Are you . . . are you really who I think you are?"

The mouth formed into a big grin. "There's a song you should listen to."

"What's that? One of yours?"

"We *are* the greatest rock and roll band in the world."

"True. What's the song?"

"'Blind Man'. Check it out."

The giant lips pursed and blew against the crest of a nearby mountain, propelling it backwards through the sky. As it disappeared over the horizon, I could distantly hear the voice, cackling with amusement. "Hey, Joe! You ain't gonna believe this one!"

119

Then

Chapter Fourteen: Learning to Chill

First time I got high, really high, I was twelve. I'd been around dope and booze every day until I got sent away to Grandma Rose's, but this was the moment when it all clicked for me. I was at the next-door neighbor's house, where I'd been baby-sitting her son, Tobey. He was down for a nap now, and Tisha was pulling out the cash to pay me with. When her hand came out of her purse, she was not just holding dollar bills; she'd accidentally pulled out a joint, as well.

When she saw me look at her hand, she looked down too, and then blushed. "Oops. Sorry about that. I mean . . . well, I'm sorry if you're offended, I guess. If you're not offended, then . . . you wanna light one up?"

Tisha was in her twenties, recently divorced, and I loved how she dressed – hip and strange and daring. She seemed like the epitome of sophistication to me at the time, and I desperately wanted her to think I was cool, too.

"Sure, I guess so." Bam. Not thinking about Bite, or my parents, or any one of a hundred stoned-out dopers from the communes. Just 'yeah, okay, fire it up, baby'. It's amazing how I could take a hundred hard-learned lessons about dope and dopers, and throw it all out the window without a moment's hesitation. *Me? Not me! I'm not like those other assholes; I'm different.* I took the joint and sucked a deep toke into my lungs.

Even that first time, pot was my friend. Didn't cough, didn't choke, just sucked in all that fragrant smoke and held it as long and as deep as I could. *Momma mia!*

120

As the smoke penetrated, first my lungs, then blood, then brain, I could feel myself smoothing out. Relaxing. Letting go of things I didn't even know had hold of my ass, until I felt them loosen their grip and slide away. For the first time in years, I actually felt like a kid, and felt like being a kid was enough. To this day, I remember having a moment of absolute clarity, and thinking, "this must be what normal people feel like all the time."

Click in my brain, and I was off to the races, never looking back, never stumbling. Because I was never one to be in for a penny when a pound was available. A lot of people who don't know any better think that drinkers and druggers do it to let loose. I don't know about everybody else, but that's not what it did for me. Sure, I ended up cutting way the hell loose, but that was just a side effect. The real thing it did was let me change how I felt. Instead of scared, or nervous, or worried or upset, that joint let me hit the reset button in my brain. And when you can control your brain through pot, or Jack, or cocaine or anything else? That's the tightest control of all. Better living through chemistry; that was my new motto.

Tisha was a great resource for pot, and once I realized how much it could do for me, I started broadening my horizons and looking with new eyes at the liquor cabinet and Grandma's medicine chest. When Grandpa Simon died, I was completely numb, thanks to better living through chemistry.

I started having sex right around then, too. Another thing that the judicious application of drugs and alcohol helped with. Right in the back seat of Kevin Cortico's piss-yellow Stingray. Not a lot of room for moving around back there, which was good, because I didn't know I was supposed to. Kevin was a good sport about it, though, and if he realized I was fucking him on a dare to prove to myself that I wasn't too scared by Bite to have a normal life,

121

he never let on.

And finally, dope opened up music for me in ways I never would have guessed. When things got too tough to deal with, I'd lie on the bed in my room and listen to music through my headphones, toking up and drifting away to someplace where everything made just a little more sense than it did on planet Earth.

I was ten feet tall and bulletproof then, and a combination of grace and stupidity kept me alive, in spite of myself. When I started working at *Whipt!*, it was like a 24-hour party. Everybody and their brother was hanging out and passing around cocaine, pot, heroin, and whatever else was handy. Blue kind of held himself above that, except with his old friends, which seemed appropriate to me; he had the final say on what got in the magazine. So by staying out of most of the party scene, he maintained a state above the influence, more or less. Which left the rest of us free to cavort around like maniacs, because all we could promise was to do our best. Final call was always Blue's, so hey. I'll try real hard for you, baby, and by the way, do you have any toot left?

Ernie Gallows was just one of the guys that went out with a bang back then. Everybody knew him, and everywhere there was some action, Ernie was around, buying drinks, offering a share of his personal stash. But don't ask him to light a smoke, because his hands shook so bad he was as likely to singe your eyebrows off as get the cigarette lit.

Once, he caught himself on fire trying to light a bowl with a pack of matches. He was wearing one of those plastic jackets that everyone was wearing back in the day, and not only did it go up in flames, it melted to his skin as it went. We were partying on a boat docked at the Detroit River, and

122

as he shrieked with pain, someone picked him up and threw him bodily off the side of the boat into the water. Bummer was, he couldn't swim.

Everyone was so stoned Ernie nearly drowned before we got him fished out, and then we kept partying for a couple more hours before he was able to bum a ride to the emergency room. Turned out he had second and third degree burns over most of his chest and arms, and had picked up a nasty infection from bobbing around in the river, on top of everything else.

But even that wasn't the real story. He was like a guy addicted to jaywalking, who can't stay out of the street, no matter how many times he gets run over. He was the one that nobody wanted to be like. The guy we all looked at and said, "if I ever get that bad, I'll quit."

I ran into him one night at Vermilion Gallery, right after Max had opened it up. He was mooching free liquor, and twitching around and whining about how he needed to cop. Crack. "Just one rock, just one," was the refrain we were all getting tired of hearing.

At one point, Ernie had been a pretty decent painter. He'd done a couple of covers for *Whipt!*, but his stuff had gotten darker and darker the further down he went, until everything he created looked like melting corpses. Not a happy place inside his head.

He grinned when he saw me come in, or at least that's what I thought he was trying to do. It looked more like a grimace, but his voice was cheery enough when he called out, "hey, Elvira! Come have a drink with me!"

"You buying?" I asked, just to bug him. We all knew he didn't have any money, ever. It all went straight into the pipe.

"That hurts, Eve. You know I'm broke this week. Rent due on the apartment, car broke down, have to take the fucking bus everywhere. . ."

123

He looked like he was gonna burst into tears of self-pity any second. "Hey, Barrio!" I called, slapping a ten spot on the bar. "Hit me and my friend, would ya?"

"Oh, thanks, Eve. It's nice that you don't forget your friends now that you got that bigshot new job and everything. How's it feel to be a star? Have everybody kissin' your ass, talking nice to you, all that shit."

I looked him over briefly, wondering if he had any idea how offensive he was. "Ernie, if you want to drink on my dime, shut the fuck up, okay?"

"Sure thing, Evie. Sure thing." I could still hear him muttering as I walked over to sit with Max. Dude couldn't shut up to save his life.

"I'm worried about him," said Max, nodding in Ernie's direction. He doesn't even make sense anymore, whether he's high or not. He's destroying brain cells fast enough to set a new land-speed record."

I glanced in Ernie's direction. "What do you give a fuck about him for, anyway? I don't even know why you let him keep coming in here. He never pays for anything, he hasn't produced a piece of art in six months. He's just another loser who used to be someone."

Max grinned at me. "I saw you buy him a drink, not two minutes ago. Why do *you* give a fuck about him, Oh Judgmental One?"

I shrugged. "I don't. I had a good day today. I would have bought your dog a drink, if you had a dog. Oh, wait, you have Paulie, don't you." Paulie was Max's current love interest, a curly-haired hanger-on who reminded me of a poodle. "Hey, Paulie, want a drink? I'm buying."

From across the room, Paulie lifted a glass to me and nodded.

"Barrio, a drink for Paulie, please." I turned back to Max. "See?"

124

Max shook his head, but he was fighting a grin. "You are a cruel, cruel woman."

"No, I'm a cruel, cruel writer. The woman part is incidental, but the writer part is essential."

Just then there was a ruckus by the door, followed by the sound of someone screeching with rage – it sounded like one of those Monty Python drag queen things, but turned out to be Ernie, who had taken offense at something someone had said to him on his way out the door.

"Hey," said Barrio, coming around the bar, baseball bat in hand. "You leave him alone. You ain't got no call to put your hands on him like that."

I looked a little closer. Sure enough, the guy who had started Ernie going looked like a minor dealer to me, complete with black leather jacket and a fedora with a red feather in it. Shit.

I stood up and walked over, Max at my side. "What's the deal here, man?"

"I been lookin' for this skanky-ass little punk for two days. He owes me some money, and I ain't waiting no longer."

Christ. This was going to seriously impact on tonight's partying. "Look at him for Christ sake. He doesn't have any money. He was in here scammin' drinks."

"Then I'm gonna have to waste him."

"Wait, wait, wait," said Max, stepping forward. "How much does he owe you?"

The man glowered at Ernie for a minute. "Two hundred dollars."

I was incredulous. "You're going to waste another human being for two hundred bucks?"

125

"Guess so."

"Nah, come on in and have a drink. Let's figure something out."

The dealer took a gun out of his pocket and shot it into the ceiling. The blast of sound got the attention of everyone in the room. Ernie peed his pants, and the smell of urine filled the air. "I don't want to *work something out* with a bunch of middle-class white asshole kids who are pretending they're tough. I want my goddamn money and I want it right now."

"Fuck," I breathed.

"I got fifty bucks on me, who else?" said Max, pulling money out of his pocket.

"I got twenty," I said. "And some change coming from Barrio."

"I got a hundred," said the bartender, leaning the baseball bat against the bar so he could get money out of his pockets.

We muttered around, collecting money, and still came up twenty dollars short. "Hey, can you hang out while I go to an ATM?" I asked.

The dealer looked at me in disbelief. "You want me to hang out with this bunch of poser assholes, while you go to an ATM and get twenty bucks to pay up this guy's tab with me? Are you fuckin' crazy?"

"Come on," I said. "It'll be cool. And it'll just take a few minutes. It's better than killing a guy, isn't it?"

He looked at me, then at the money in Max's hand. Then at Ernie. "Tell you what. You give me the cash you have right now, and I shoot him in the foot."

"What?" squeaked Ernie.

"What?" I asked.

The dealer sighed. "You give me the cash now, and I don't kill him.

126

But I got to do something, I can't just say I'm gonna kill him if he don't come up with the money and then let him walk with a partial payment. That's not right."

"So, we give you a hundred-eighty dollars, and you shoot him in the foot on principle?"

"That's it." He smiled at me, apparently pleased that I'd gotten it.

"Sounds good to me," I said. "Ernie, put your goddamn foot out here and let's get this over with."

Ernie answered by making a dash for the door, but his dealer stuck out a foot and tripped him, then wrenched him off of the floor and sat him up on the bar. "Motherfucker, I wasted enough time tryin' to track you down. Don't you dare make me chase you out this door."

He shook Ernie like the junkie was some kind of scruffy cat. "You got me, boy?"

"Yeah, I got you."

The dealer set him down on his feet, and drew a bead on Ernie's left foot.

"Wait!" It was Ernie.

"Wait for what?" asked the guy with the gun.

"I . . . I might have twenty dollars," said Ernie.

"Motherfucker, you better not be lying to me. Where is it?"

"In my pocket."

"Don't you reach for it. I'll get it." The dealer stuck his hand in Ernie's front pocket and pulled out a wad of bills. Three, four hundred dollars, easy. We all gasped with amazement. Ernie looked embarrassed.

"Man, you had the money all the time," said the guy with the gun.

127

"Why didn't you just pay me? Why did you let all your friends come up with the money for you, when you had it all the time?"

Ernie shrugged and looked up at the dealer from under his eyebrows. "If I did that, how was I gonna cop later?"

Before anyone else could react, I pulled my brand new Glock out of my bag.

Then I shot that skanky motherfuckin' Ernie in the foot myself.

Now

Chapter Fifteen: Heard the One About the Really Fat Priest?

Next morning was ass-kickingly beautiful. Sun shining, birds singing, the Wild Men making enough bacon and eggs to block the arteries of the entire state of California, when Puck came staggering out of his cabin, looking a little the worse for wear. He blinked blearily at us as we set up a breakfast table outside.

"Hey, Antlers!" called Dicker. "Come on over and have some breakfast!" His men were scurrying about on his orders, jockeying in macho fashion for who would have the honor of kissing ass on the boss next.

Puck looked at him, vaguely astonished. Then he looked at me. "Hey, sorry about the whole I-gave-acid-to-your-grandma thing. But what's up with these guys?"

I shrugged and kept setting out plates. "Don't know. Maybe they finally got in touch with their inner manliness."

"I can see that, but how?"

"Maybe it was the LSD and the Jack Daniels. Or maybe it was the strip poker. Dicker was a big winner last night."

Puck looked impressed. "He got you naked?"

I laughed. "No, *Grandma* got *him* naked. The other guys were just impressed that he survived it."

"Me, too," said Puck, eying Grandma Rose cautiously. "I've got a group of blow-dryer execs coming in next week. Think she'd be interested in sticking around?"

129

I shook my head. "We're women on a mission, *Antlers*. But I'll let her know you want her to keep in touch."

Just then, two of the guys got into a loud wrestling match, and everyone gathered around to cheer them on, hollering obscene and colorful encouragement. When they both picked themselves up from the ground and shook off the dust, grinning, a loud cheer went up.

Puck shook his head. "Still – whoa – you know what I mean? I'll give her my card. Don't let her lose it, okay? Just, you know, in case."

*

After breakfast, we packed up our gear and headed back out, down to Ruby's to drop off our key, then back to the highway and on to Laughlin, Nevada, Sinner's Paradise. It was a gambling town, sort of like Vegas, but about a quarter of the size, and sat on a fat, lazy river where you could ride paddle wheel boats if you didn't want to shop, gamble or watch floor shows. Grandma Rose was elated; I was bored out of my skull, and getting nervous about exactly how I was going to go about hooking up with Tyler when we hit Los Angeles. We had listened to *Blind Man* about fifty times on the way from Bryce to Laughlin, but neither one of us had been able to figure out what it was supposed to mean, or portend or commentate on or whatever, so that was completely useless as far as I could see.

Grandma Rose decided the first thing she wanted to do in Laughlin was hit the Strip and gamble away some money, producing a dental mirror that she was gonna use in some nefarious scheme to rob the other gamblers blind; but I was in some major turmoil, and decided to go hang out in this long, skinny park that paralleled the river. Life, and all the hits that were coming at me, was going faster than I could keep up with, to the point where

130

I was actually questioning my entire life, lifestyle and purpose. I was actually more than half believing that some LSD-fueled dream held the key to my future, and I didn't know if I was more scared that it would or would not turn out to be true. If it was all real, I had a fucking boatload of stuff to make up for, and if it wasn't, I was totally, rat's ass alone in the universe, except for Max and Grandma Rose. I sat there as the air cooled and the sun grew bigger and redder, and still didn't know what the hell I was going to do.

Until I saw a blind guy, who looked even scrawnier and dirtier than skanky Ernie Gallows used to, tapping his way through the park. I got up from my bench and circled him twice before I moved to intercept. Butterflies I hadn't known existed were going nuts trying to escape my stomach through my throat.

"Excuse me, sir?"

"What? What's that?" Great. Not only blind, but deaf, too.

"My name is Eve." Okay, now what? Do you know anything about talking clouds? You holding a secret message for me from the Acid-Trip Gods? I decided to postpone the moment where I let him know I was totally crazed. "Listen. You look like you could use a meal. You hungry?"

He licked toothless gums. "Where you wanna go eat at?"

"I don't know, pops. What's good around here?"

He tilted his head up, as if he was smelling the air for the direction of his next meal. "You're buying, right?"

"Right."

"There's a Sizzler right around the corner. That okay?"

"I guess I could swing that. Come on, hot guy. Let's get some food."

"Did you know all the homeless chicks dig me?"

131

"No, but I shoulda guessed."

*

Over dinner, I tried to explain it to him. He'd pulled out a pair of teeth from his pants pocket, and was enjoying the hell out of his steak, but I could tell he wasn't too impressed with me. "You had a damn dream that some guy with big lips was telling you to listen to a song about a blind man, and you think that means you gotta buy me dinner and then I'll give you some advice? Sweetheart, that's the dumbest thing I ever heard."

It didn't help much that he was shouting his opinion at the top of his lungs. Everyone in the Sizzler turned to see what the old guy was yelling about.

"Could you please keep your frickin' voice down?"

"What?" Apparently, he couldn't.

"Look, tell me something. Don't worry about it, just tell me *something*. I'll figure out what it means."

He ran a piece of biscuit around his plate and then sucked it off his fingers. "Well, I'll tell you this. If I was gonna give some advice, the advice would be to talk to someone who gives a shit. Which ain't me, although I do thank you for dinner. There's a priest that comes to the park in the evenings, sometimes. He's a good man to talk to. Why don't you go look for him?"

He smiled, and for just a second, his face changed and became almost beautiful. "Go find that priest, young lady. He'll help you figure out what to do next."

"I don't suppose you know what he looks like?"

The old guy started guffawing so hard I thought he was gonna choke. "Oh, that's a good one. Now pay the bill and get the hell out of here. I

132

can find my own way home."

I did what he told me, and tucked an extra twenty into his pocket for next time. Then I headed back to the park.

As I walked back, I flashed back on some of the messages that had been coming my way lately, and how I was starting to think that some of them were . . . well, could be . . . maybe . . . spot on. I wasn't sure what exactly I was supposed to do with the priest, but I had a sneaking suspicion. If he was cool, I might run some of this by him and see what he thought. I needed someone more objective than Grandma Rose and Max. Maybe. Possibly.

*

Sure enough, as I wandered around in the dusky twilight, I found a guy in a priest's outfit sitting on a bench. He had the black linen suit and shirt, along with the little white cardboard thingee tucked under his collar instead of a tie. The thing that threw me – aside from getting fired, prophetic clouds and oracular blind homeless guys – was that he was built like a refrigerator, and he was Oriental. I always thought of priests as skinny Irish guys, except when they were skinny and Italian – somewhere in between George Carlin and Al Pacino. I circled him a couple of times before I decided to get closer, wondering what I was gonna hear *this* time that I didn't like.

I approached the bench, and he eyed me warily. "Are you thinking about trying to mug me? Because I know martial arts, and I can fold you up and toss you under a bus faster than you can say 'hail Mary,'" he warned.

"Really?"

"Well, no. But you do look kind of scary just circling me like that, and everyone in America thinks that if you have an epicanthic fold, you have to know martial arts."

133

I sat down on the bench next to him. "Sorry about that. A lot of people think I'm kinda scary even if I'm not circling them. You're the priest that the blind man told me about, right?"

"Old guy? Looks like he's gonna keel over any second?"

"That's him."

"And he told you to go look for the big chink priest in the park. How many fat Oriental guys do you think are hanging around in this park wearing clerical garb, young lady?"

"Okay, right. Sorry, I'm just a little nervous. Listen, do you have a few minutes?"

He sighed. I wasn't actually Catholic, but I'd seen enough movies to know what came next. I told him everything. From killing Bite with the poker to kneeing Jay in the balls to calling the pastor a dumb fuck in front of his whole congregation, to shooting Ernie in the foot, walking out on Blue and setting Loyola's desk on fire.

When I was all done, we sat in silence for a few moments, until I got restless enough to ask, "Okay, so now what?"

"Now what, what?" he countered.

"Aren't you supposed to give me some directions, or stuff to do for penance or something?"

"Seriously?"

Now I was getting irritated. "Come on, Father. I don't have all night here. My Grandma is out there gambling her ass off somewhere, using a dental mirror to peek at other peoples' cards, and I'm gonna have to go find her and drag her off to bed before the casino managers get wise."

"It's the Catholics that give out penance. Not the Third Church."

"What do you mean, 'it's the Catholics?' Aren't you Catholic?"

"No, I just said. I'm Samoan. From the Third Church of Samoa. We're a lot more easy going. Except for the collar thing."

"You tricked me into thinking you were a Catholic priest," I said, rising to my feet, panicked. Did this mean I'd have to do the whole thing all over again?

He put two meaty palms out in a pacifying gesture. "Hey, how was I supposed to know what you wanted? Anyone who starts a confession with, 'Dude, I've done some bad shit and I want to talk to you about it,' doesn't strike me as being a stickler for rules."

I snorted. "I want some damn penance."

"Okay," he said, thinking. "Look, I got a friend who's a priest – a *Catholic* one. I'll call him on my cell phone and find out what he would say. Just give me a minute, okay?"

Calmer, I sat back down on the bench and listened while he made the call. It took a while, and he ended up sending me across the street to an all-night drugstore for a notepad and a pen so he could write it all down, but finally, he flipped the phone shut and turned to me, notepad in hand.

"Okay," he said. "We got some work to do." He gestured with the notepad. "Now, as far as I can tell, this is a list of the acts you need penance for: First, murder; second shooting that guy in the foot; third being disrespectful to your mother and father; fourth—"

"My mother and father were assholes, they deserved everything I did to them," I said. "And how about what they did to me?"

He looked at me and his eyes narrowed. He really did look like a priest. "Look, you want *them* to get right, or *you*? Cause if you're concerned

135

about saving your own ass, it doesn't matter what they deserved. Let God take care of that. You focus on what you did, little sister. That's how this thing works."

"But . . ."

"No."

"Yeah, but. . ."

"No, no, no. Now you ready to get on with this or not?"

I sulked, but agreed. It was sorta funny, really. Now that I'd told him, it was his responsibility, right? He picked up where he had left off.

"Fourth, fornication. A *lot* of fornication. Fifth, cursing."

"What about the drinking and stuff?"

He waved a hand. "Odd but true, God's okay with that. According to my friend. Keep in mind he's Catholic, though. You might want to check that with someone else. Can I keep going? I got a service to conduct in the morning. Okay? Sixth, stealing cash from your grandmother's purse when you were ten. Seventh, setting four different receptionists' desks on fire, and one receptionist. Eighth. . ." and on it went.

Once he had the list down to his own satisfaction, he turned to me and put his hand on my forehead. "I have listened to the confession of your sins, both mortal and venal," he intoned. "I extend to you the forgiveness of The Father, the Son and the Holy Ghost. Go forth, my child, and sin no more."

He took his hand off my head and sat there, beaming at me.

"That's it?"

"What do you mean, 'that's it?' What exactly did you expect? The heavens were gonna part and a bunch of little cherubim were going to swoop down and pat you on the back or something?"

136

"No, I expected you to give me a list of stuff to do to make it right, and I was gonna bitch about it a while, then go do it, and all would be forgiven."

He shook his head. "Honey, there is *nothing* you can do to get rid of this stuff." He held up the notepad to make his point. "Either God's going to get you for it or not. What you can do is try to balance it all out by either making it right if you can, or making something else right in it's place if there's no way to fix the original thing anymore. Now, my suggestion is try to get your shit together, and be a good girl while God decides whether you got some grace left with him or not."

He studied me for a moment. "Here. Take this list. Go find your Grandma, go back to your hotel room, and when the time seems right, I want you to get down on your knees, pray to Tagaloa to return your soul to harmony with the waters – and *mean* it. Then you get up off your knees, and start doing the next right thing. Make a list of everyone you've harmed, and figure out what you can do to fix it. Then do that.

"Now, regarding this Bite guy. When I'm talking about making it right with the people you've harmed, I'm not talking about confessing to the police. You didn't harm them. Probably helped prevent God knows what else. But there's other kids out there. Get my drift? Don't kill anyone else, though. Or shoot anyone. Even in the foot. You're a grownup now; figure out some other way. Not once in a while, not when you feel like it. Every single time. You got a lot of making up for to do, so I suggest you go out there and get busy."

"Huh. Is this what the Catholic dude told you to tell me?"

He gave me a smile full of sunshine and crashing waves. "Nah, this is from

137

me. It'll work."

"You're sure? How will I know what He wants me to do?"

"I'm sure. Look. God's either real or he's not. Forget about what people tell you, look for what he shows you. Keep your eye on the ball, not the pitcher. Go. Now."

"Okay," I said, standing up. Unexpectedly, I felt light-hearted and happy. I held my arms out and did a twirl. Okay. Maybe not *that* happy. But still, happy. I started to kiss him, then thought better of it and held out a hand to shake.

He nodded approvingly. "Good save. Go have a life. Remember, don't kill anyone else, don't shoot anyone in the foot, and try to watch the language, okay? Ride the waves, don't fight 'em. And don't forget to look for the next right thing."

"Got it. No killing, no shooting, less swearing, more surfing. Metaphorically on the surfing, of course."

I ran back to the hotel we had started at, found Grandma Rose, and we proceeded to get rip-roaring drunk in the hotel bar. Then, just in case, I tipped the waitress really well.

*

When Grandma Rose went to sleep that night, I got down on my knees, just like the priest had said. "Okay, dude, this is it," I said. "You want me to do something different, you're gonna have to show me what it is, cause I'm willing, but I have no idea what I'm doing."

I waited a minute, but the only response I got was from Grandma Rose. "Eve? What the hell are you doing over there?"

"I'm . . . praying?"

"Huh. Why? You get converted or something this afternoon when I wasn't looking?" I could see her outline as she sat up in bed in the dark room and peered at me. "Are you one of those born-again Christians, all of a sudden?"

"No, I don't think so. I think I'm a Samosa now."

She grunted. "Aren't Samosas Girl Scout cookies?"

The thought made me laugh and forget I was waiting for divine enlightenment. "I think so. That and surfers."

"Go to sleep, Evie. God Bless."

"You, too, Grandma Rose."

139

Then

Chapter Sixteen: Dark Dreams

About the time puberty had fully embraced me in its sweaty grasp, I started having nightmares every night. I'd dream of Bite's face, of my mother sobbing in spacey terror, of my father lying outside Bite's door leaking big fat tears of self pity. I'd wake up shaking and wanting to scream. Or I'd conjure up Jay's leering face, his hard hands squeezing my breasts while I squirmed and tried to get away. If those images didn't work to scare the living shit out of me, there was always one of Studder floating on the water in the gravel pit, bloated and rotten.

Sleep was not a friend of mine.

Fortunately, Max wasn't much for sleeping at night, either. We'd call each other and talk until one or the other of us drifted off to sleep. Later, when we both had computers and Internet hookups, we'd IM each other until the sky started to turn pink. Speed helped a lot to stay awake during school, and then I'd catch up on the weekend. It also helped me get rid of the rest of the baby fat I was carrying around.

From the late-night chats with Max grew my column. They were always intimate, addressed inside my head to Max.

From the speed grew my enchantment with cocaine, which was not only cleaner and more chic than speed, but made me feel . . . *right.* Confident, illuminated, powerful.

I had gone with Max to party at the house of this girl we copped from a lot. There were probably fifty or sixty people crammed into a modest brick two story off of Five Mile Road. Music was blaring, and there was

140

cocaine everywhere. Practically everyone there was a young somebody – artist, musician, fashionista, whatever. Having a good time, groovin' on the music.

We had moved on from snorting lines to freebasing, which I'm told is a lot like smokin' crack. I was standing in the kitchen with Isis. Isis. I know it was silly, but she was a model, and determined to carve out a one-name-only-niche for herself. Plus she had all the coke. There was a bottle of 151 rum on the table next to the bong-thing we were using, and everyone was pretty damn focused, including me. I don't think I'd smiled in an hour. Max was standing next to me, grinding his teeth. All of a sudden, the front door flies open with a crash that shook the whole damn house. People started fleeing immediately, the paranoid fucks. But it wasn't a cop that came barreling into the kitchen, screaming something I couldn't quite make out. It sounded like, "where's it at?", over and over, while he slammed cabinet doors and threw dishes.

"What the fuck is he looking for?" I turned to Isis, who was watching him ruefully.

"His coke stash," she whispered. "He does it all, then he gets crazy and starts thinking somebody took some of it and hid it here. There's not really a lot I can do until he winds down, except . . ."

While he was bending over and inspecting the inside of the oven, she grabbed a frying pan and bashed him over the head. He collapsed on the open door of the oven. Isis looked at him thoughtfully and gave him a nudge. He didn't stir.

"Can you guys get him out of there and put him somewhere else? It's a gas oven," she explained. "Or we could just let him lay."

141

Several of the guys pitched in to pick him up, but he was a hefty guy, and they ended up just dragging him into a corner and letting go.

The music kept blaring, the party kept going, the brother kept dripping blood out of his nose onto dirty linoleum. I turned to Max, who looked a little green. "You ready? I'm freakin' out here."

He nodded, and when we got outside, he gulped deep breaths of smoggy air in the moonlight. "I don't think I want to do this anymore, Eve. I quit."

"Yeah," I said, starting up the car and pulling away from the curb with the caution that proceeds the crossover into sloppy drunkenness. "Me too."

And we did, substituting more alcohol for coke and speed. I hadn't realized how stuck on it I was, until my nightmares stopped being the thing that was keeping me awake, and it started being the howl of cocaine, stalking me in the dark.

Now

Chapter Seventeen:
The Land of Pixie Dust and Protozoa

The next morning, we woke up lazy, had breakfast, dropped a few more quarters in the slots, and then took off for LA. We were both dressed for California weather, Grandma Rose in a flowery sun dress and sandals, while I had given up the black leather in favor of cut-offs, tennis shoes and an Hawaiian shirt. I'd braided my hair against the ravages of the convertible, and I called Twinkie's daughter Pixie on my cell phone as we were leaving town.

She sounded like a pixie, sparkling and full of secret amusement. She lived in a little small suburb of Los Angeles called Citrus Heights, so we made plans to head there first, have dinner and crash for the night before we went out in search of Steven Tyler.

The sun was shining and the top was down, so I cranked up the CD player, and we sang along at the top of our lungs while we shot through the desert. While I was singing, I was also thinking. We were nearly at the end of the road, and I wasn't sure I was ready to end it. I didn't know what to make of my old life anymore.

Maybe I had been acting angry 'cause I felt scared. Maybe I had been stuck in a rut. Maybe all the partying hadn't been as much fun as it was supposed to be. Maybe some of it had been desperation. Fuck it. Introspection was not my strong suit.

I shrugged and decided to stop thinking for a while. I was on the way now, to wherever the hell I was going, and I was feeling pretty damn

143

light and breezy. Sitting next to me, Grandma Rose didn't seem to have noticed my introspection, so I tuned back into the music and sang a little louder, my voice getting whipped back by the warm wind into my ears and off into the ether. The tune was "Crazy", which seemed pretty fitting.

By this time, Grandma Rose knew the lyrics to every Aerosmith song I had brought, nearly as well as I did. We got almost all the way through 1993's *Get a Grip*, and I reached over to pop it out before "Amazing" started. Okay song, I guess, and people made a big fuss about Alicia Silverstone when the video came out, but it never did much for me, personally. I don't think I'd ever listened to it all the way through. Sounded like a dirge at the beginning.

Grandma Rose reached out and put a hand on mine just before I hit the open button. "What's your hurry? Let me listen to this."

"It sucks."

"So, let me find out for myself."

I sighed, but it was just for show. "Okay, Rosie-O, don't get your panties in a bunch." I removed my finger from the vicinity of the button that would have ejected the disc, and sat back for a few minutes of ear torture.

It didn't sound so bad, though, this time. Reminded me a little bit of "Blind Man," to tell you the truth. I started getting sucked into the lyrics. Grandma Rose was my angel of mercy, I thought, humming. Or Max. I wondered what Max would think if I told him I thought of him as an angel. And everything that had happened since we started this road trip had been pretty amazing.

The song ended, and I reached out to the CD player.

"There's another song on there," Grandma Rose pointed out.

"I need to hear this one again, first," I said, hitting repeat.

144

For the next two hours, we listened to "Amazing" over and over and over while ideas percolated through my head at light-speed. Epiphany. An epiphany is what it was. I'd had some limited experience with epiphanies before, but nothing like this. I felt like my brain was gonna explode, or my heart, but a good explode, I thought. I laid my hand on the armrest between us, and Grandma Rose clasped it with one of her own, and we learned every word.

When we finally reached the Citrus Hills exit, I hit stop, and the silence boomed in my head. I looked at Grandma Rose. "I don't want to be a desperate heart anymore, Grandma."

She looked at me and smiled. "I think your moment's rushing toward you, Eve."

I shivered a little, excitement and fear mixed together. What the hell would I do if I did have the moment? Would it change everything? Would it change me? Whatever the hell was gonna happen, I hoped it hurried the fuck up. Waiting was never something I was very good at.

Shrugging, I picked the piece of paper I'd written Pixie's directions on, and handed it to Grandma Rose. "You're the navigator, where to?" Then I whipped back onto the road.

*

Pixie's house was a cobbled cottage that looked like it belonged on a rocky cost in Maine, instead of one long swoop down to the sunny Pacific. She had two roommates, one of whom was grinding coffee beans in the kitchen when we arrived. The other one was due home soon.

Just like her mom, Pixie turned out to be a really *large* girl. She must have weighed nearly as much as her mother, with long, wild gold hair that

145

reached nearly to her waist, and a freedom in her movements that made her eye-catching despite her poundage.

Pixie bubbled over with humor, and with a sly wit that reminded me of Quisp. She was dressed in calf-high, black Doc Martens and a short, wispy dress, and acted as happy to see us as if we were old friends she had invited herself. Her face was clear of makeup and she had that scrubbed clean, earnest skin that came with being just barely of age.

Her roommate was pierced and studded and dyed and had enough eyeliner slathered on to look like she'd just walked out of a club anywhere in Detroit. In deference to the weather, she was wearing black mesh instead of black leather, but the intent was plain.

Pixie and Sam, the black mesh girl, started dinner while Grandma Rose and I sat at the kitchen table, kibitzing and peeling vegetables. Pixie dug out a bottle of sake to go with the stir-fry they were putting together, and Grandma popped Aerosmith into Pixie's player.

"Jesus Christ," said Sam, when it started up. "Who is that?"

"Aerosmith. We're going to meet 'em tomorrow. I'm going to ply Steven Tyler with sexual favors so that he'll explain the meaning of life to Evie." Grandma beamed around the kitchen.

Sam poured herself another shot of sake and tossed it down. "Well. At least they're in your age group."

"I beg your pardon?" said Grandma, sounding a trifle put out.

"Come on, Mrs. . . . Mrs. . . ."

"Rose," said Grandma firmly.

"Anyway, Rose," continued Sam. "Those guys must be two-hundred years old by now."

146

Grandma's brow darkened, and I winced. But she smiled disarmingly. "And if they're in my age group, that would make me at least two hundred years old, too, right?"

I snickered, and she shot me a dangerous look, so I did my shot of sake and tried to keep a straight face.

Pixie giggled, and Grandma took her eyes off Sam, to Sam's apparent relief, in order to pin Pixie with the same glare she'd turned on me. Instead of shutting up, though, Pixie winked at Grandma. "Which would make you the most experienced woman at the table today. Why don't you give us a few pointers?"

"Well, I guess I am," said Grandma Rose, looking surprised. "But you girls are awful young. I'm not sure you're ready to hear what I've learned in sixty years of bagging the beanies."

"Banging the what?" I asked.

"Baggin' the beanies," she said. "You know. Waterin' the beanpole. Raising the flag. The horizontal hokey pokey. Serenading the sausage."

"Is that anything like bumpin' uglies?" Sam said.

"Or playing hide the salami?" Pixie added.

"How about stirrin' up the jean juice?" I tossed in.

"Docking the spaceship," countered Sam.

"Getting the kink out of the Kaiser," said Grandma, which stopped us all for a minute.

"Frosting the strudel," said Pixie, and we were all off again.

The stir-fry was going, and we did another round of sake shooters while Grandma launched into an account of our trip. She'd just gotten to the Emerald City, when the front door opened and another girl walked in. I

147

assumed she was the missing roommate.

"Oh, my," she said, in a breathless voice. "Something smells really yummy!"

Of the three of them, she was the only one who looked like a co-ed. Burnished strawberry blond hair, as long and curly as a Barbie Doll's, pretty makeup over a creamy complexion, a crisp pink blouse over a short plaid skirt. She looked like she should be doing the Pope wave from the back of a convertible at the Rose Bowl.

"This is Adelaide, our other roommate," said Pixie. Sam walked over and kissed her on the lips, a kiss that was returned warmly by the little homecoming queen. "We call her Addy. She's majoring in marine biology."

Huh. I would have figured shopping. Buying. Whatever it was all the celebutants were interested in this year.

"What's your major, Pixie?" asked Grandma Rose, slurring just a little in the warm befuddlement of her sake.

"Aerospace engineering."

"Wow!" I said, really impressed. I turned to Sam. "How about you?"

She looked at her toes. "Accounting."

Addy put a warm hand on her shoulder. "That's nothing to be ashamed of, Sam. You should be proud of what you're doing. If it wasn't for accounting, all those spaceships would never get off the ground. The sea turtles would never get saved. Accounting makes the world go around."

Sam gave her a sappy look.

"I think the expression is, 'money makes the world go around'," I said, quite reasonably.

Addy shook her head like I was a kid who had just told her the moon

148

was made of green cheese. "Money doesn't do anything without someone to keep track of it, distribute it and deposit it," she corrected me gently. "And Sammy is our girl for that. She's gonna make accounting *rock*. Now, what were you guys all laughing about before I came in?"

Grandma took up the story where she had left off, Pixie got back on the stir-fry, and Addy got busy making up for lost sake.

*

By the time dinner was over, we were all pretty loose, and Grandma Rose had everybody up to date. After we cleared off the table and oozed our way into the kitchen, Addy said, "You know, I don't think I've ever heard that song you're talking about. Amazing? Do you have it with you?"

"You've never heard it?" I asked, slightly incredulous.

"I don't think I've ever heard that band you're talking about, either. At least, if I did, it was by accident, and I didn't know it was them. You know?"

Now I was gaping. "What the hell kind of music do you listen to?"

She gave me the thousand-watt smile and snuggled closer to Sam.

"Country?" She didn't even have the sense to look embarrassed.

Sam said defensively, "She comes from Kentucky."

Oh, well. That explained it all. A corn-belt lesbian marine biologist who listened to country while she was dissecting penguins and picking out prom dresses. What was *I* thinking?

Grandma Rose picked up her bag, which had our CDs in it. She rifled though and after a minute, pulled out *Get a Grip* and a couple of joints.

"Is that what I think it is?" asked Pixie, looking delighted.

Sam sat forward, a look of mild interest on her face. "That's pot,

149

right?"

"What's pot?" asked Addy.

"Marijuana, silly," replied Sam.

Addy giggled. "I didn't know people still had that."

Pixie nodded as Grandma fired one up. "I haven't seen pot since seventh grade."

Before anyone else could say anything incomprehensible and ridiculous, I popped in the CD and forwarded to "Amazing", then cranked the volume. Grandma passed the joint, but I decided to pass. The sake was already making it hard to think, and for some crazy reason, thinking seemed more important than getting fucked up. Go figure.

Everyone listened until the song ended, and I clicked pause. "I don't get it," said Addy.

"Me either," said Sam.

"I'm not entirely sure, either," I confessed. "But every time I hear it, I get the feeling that I'm balancing right on the edge of something. It's the same feeling I get when I look at the singer's face. Like the key's in the lock, just waiting for me to give it a good crank. This whole trip's been about getting real, getting ready to turn the key. I didn't realize that when we left, but I'm starting to get it now."

"It's you," said Pixie. "But you have to turn the key by *doing* something, not thinking about it."

"What the hell does that mean?"

"Jesus, Eve. You're the one who's been stuck. You *thought* you were in control the whole time, but you couldn't 'get out the door' until you got shoved out. Then you started to figure out how much you'd been bullshitting yourself all along."

"Yeah, okay, I can see that," said Sam, nodding her head. "It's all there in front of you, but you're going to have to figure out what to do next to make the key turn."

She and Pixie beamed at me like I was a child almost ready to tie her shoes for the first time.

I snorted. "Fuck that. You guys are talking in circles. Yack, yack, yack. Tell me something that makes sense, or knock it off."

At that moment, Addy perked up. "You're like a pearl, Eve. You know how pearls are made?"

"Yeah. They start with a grain of sand that gets into the oyster's shell. It irritates the oyster, who squirts out some gunk to coat it with. Liquid pearl. The pearl stuff hardens, but sooner or later, the little lump irritates the oyster some more, so it squirts out some more gunk. Eventually, bam! A pearl."

"Exactly," said Addy, tucking a strand of long, blond hair behind her ear and looking earnest. "You have a grain of sand that got stuck inside you, and you've shaped everything else in your life around it ever since. You're so used to it, that it feels normal, but it's not. You're not geared to have new experiences, you just keep re-living old ones juxtaposed on whatever's happening today."

"Wow, babe," said Sam. "That was really deep."

"I know," said Addy shyly. "Thank you. I'm minoring in the psychology of invertebrates. There's a lot we can learn from our spineless friends."

Before I could give her my opinion, Pixie hopped up and popped in a new CD. Her face was glowing with sake and excitement. "You know what I

151

feel like?"

"What?" said Grandma Rose.

"A panty dance! In the moonlight!" With that, she dragged her dress off over her head and danced her way to the door in the kitchen, leading to the backyard.

Addy and Sam both leaped up to follow her lead, and Grandma and I followed too, me despite the fact that she had put in the Pussycat Dolls. Grandma, it hardly needs to be said, got out of her clothes faster than I did, even though she had a ton more of them. That's what happens with 40 years of extra practice, I guess.

We were dancing away on the patio, Pussycat Girls blaring, and when the CD ended and our ears were ringing, Pixie looked at me and bellowed, "You've got really nice tits, Eve."

"You have really ginormous ones, Pixie." Honest to God.

Then Grandma hollered, "And mine are aged like fine wine. Wanna see?"

She made to unhook her bra and I lunged for her hands. "No! Grandma! It's okay."

She pouted, then her face cleared, and she said, "can any of you do this?"

Grandma bent over at the hip, impossibly far, until her head was parallel to her knees. Then she locked her arms around her neck and looked at us through her legs, smiling upside down.

"Wow," said Addy. "That's really impressive, Rose."

"I'll say," added Pixie.

Grandma straightened up, face pinking slightly, and staggered to a chair. "I know," she said as she sat down. "That's the move that gets me all the dates at the senior center." We couldn't top that one, so we got in the hot tub instead.

When we got back to our room, I powered up the laptop and wrote Max. *I think I may be going crazy,* I typed. *I turned down free liquor and a joint, both on the same night. And you know what? It was totally cool. You think there's something wrong with me?*

Back in Detroit, it was nearly four o'clock in the morning. I stared at my email for a while, but no response from Max was forthcoming, so I powered down and went to bed.

Now

Chapter Eighteen: Night Sparks

I should have passed right out that night, considering how much sake we'd all put away, but I think the hot tub had sweated some of it out, not to mention the fact that I quit early. So I lay there, tossing and turning and remembering the past.

Maybe Addy and her oyster-psych was right. Maybe Bite was my grain of sand. Pretty big grain, but it was an analogy. Or maybe I had a few grains of sand. Bite, my parents, blah, blah, blah. But what was my metaphorical pearl, then? I had a sneaking suspicion it was everything on my list of confessions in the park, along with drinking, a little bit of paranoia, and an anger potent enough to lash out at anyone who peeked inside at the fear behind it.

Oh, fuck me. I flopped dramatically onto my back, and stared at the ceiling. Grandma Rose let out a snore, but otherwise, I didn't impress anyone.

So how do you peel back the pearl? There, I was at a loss. I was walking around with enough new self-knowledge to make my butt itch, and not an idea in the world what to do with it. I sighed and turned on my side and scowled at the wall. Blank wall. How does a person redesign their self? When did enlightenment tip over into something new?

I closed my eyes and started reciting the lyrics to every Aerosmith song I knew. Eventually, I fell asleep.

In my dream, I was back at the rim of the canyon in Bryce. The God cloud was back on the horizon, and drawing rapidly closer. It didn't look quite so stormy this time.

"So," said God, when the cloud arrived.

"So what?"

"You've finally got your shit together. You've confessed, you've been forgiven. How does it feel?"

"I still feel fucked up."

The cloud started to swell, and I rolled my eyes. *Here we go again.*

"No you don't. You're just stubborn."

"Seriously. I don't feel as good as you think I should. Something still seems . . . unfinished."

"It's because you didn't go to a real priest."

"You got something against the Samosas?"

The cloud hemmed and hawed, and finally said. "They're just kind of new to the business. Maybe you'd have more luck if you went to someone who was part of a company that was a little more established."

"Are you kidding? You know how hard that was?"

"Nonsense. Either you got the wrong guy for the job, or you left out something important."

Now, I was pissed. "Are you kidding me? That was the hardest thing I'd ever done. Once is enough."

Before the big cloud could start lecturing me again, the other cloud I'd talked to at Bryce rolled up. "Hey! Did you listen to that song?"

I gave the first cloud one last glare before I answered. "Yeah."

"Find the blind man?"

"Yep. And confessed to the priest he told me about. This other cloud doesn't think I did a good enough job."

"Did it completely suck and turn out to be the hardest thing you've

155

ever done?"

"Yes!" I was elated.

"Relax, then, you did it right."

The first cloud sank into a sullen silence.

"And," said the second cloud, "are you ready to put it into action?"

Huh. I'd kind of forgotten about the whole set-it-right thing.

"I'm not sure. I don't feel ready or anything for that yet. Don't I have to be ready, first?"

A ripple went through the cloud. Laughter. "That's a good one. You don't change how you feel by reading shit, or thinking deep thoughts. You change how you act, and the *action* changes how you feel. If you stick with it. Sorry, kid, but nothin' changes if nothin' changes. You're doing a hell of a job, though. Keep it up."

The first cloud had departed while I was talking with the second cloud. As I watched, the second cloud scudded off at high speed. Last thing I heard him say was, "Hey, Joe, how much longer you gonna be on the cell phone for man? We got a rehearsal to do."

Past, Present, Future
Chapter Nineteen: Journey's End

I woke up early, but felt slow and groggy, thanks to my mostly sleepless night, and dosed myself by heading to the kitchen, where I guzzled coffee and listened to "Amazing" turned down low. I replayed the dream in my head while I listened. A shot of sake crossed my mind, just to get the gears turning, but it was just a fleeting thought; I'd been hiding in the bottle way too much, lately, so I settled for more coffee.

When Pixie showed up in the kitchen, I looked up and watched as she got a cup out of the cabinet and poured coffee in.

Sitting down at the table, she sighed with pleasure as she took the first sip. "I love days when the coffee's ready the instant I walk into the kitchen."

She sat down with a coffee cup in front of her, and cocked her head to listen to the music. "Figure anything out yet?"

I nodded, sipping coffee and listening. Today was the day. I powered up my laptop at the kitchen table. It was time to get hold of some of those people on my list, and start setting things straight. Blue, Loyola and Freddy Yak were first. *Blue*, I wrote. *I need to tell you how sorry I am that I turned my back on what happened in Galveston. I wasn't very honest with you, and .*

. .

That done, I felt surprisingly better. Time to get on with it. According to a friend of Pixie's, who had the order for silk- screened Aerosmith tee-shirts for the band's marketing department, Aerosmith would be at a press conference at GameBuddies' LA office, announcing a new video game based

157

on the band, that afternoon. They'd be sticking around to do a benefit for a women's shelter the next day, and then a meet-and-greet at the end of the week for their record label. Three opportunities. I'd only need one.

Pixie had to go into LA, so she said we could follow her in to the GameBuddies office. After that, we were on our own, but she gave us a house key and told us she would expect us when she saw us.

Following Pixie in her little white Toyota, we took the interstate in, absentmindedly admiring the scenery. But when we crested a hill and I saw all of LA spread out before us, ocean endless beyond it, my mouth dropped open and I forgot everything but that amazing view.

Grandma Rose said, "Oh, my God, Eve, look at that!"

I nodded, then pulled it together. "Yeah, beautiful, huh? All that city and all that ocean?"

"Not the view," she said, impatiently. "Look!"

Following her pointing finger, I saw a huge billboard right next to the highway, about half a mile away. On it . . . was *me*. In my favorite pose, the cover shot on the conference table. Above the picture, in letters ten feet high, it said: *LA Wants a Taste of Eve!*

I braked and pulled off to the side of the highway, ending up behind Pixie, who had done the same. I realized belatedly that there was a huge crowd of people gathered under the billboard. Grandma Rose and I looked at each other, baffled. I shut off the Roadster, and we sat there, just looking.

After a minute, I turned and gave her a suspicious look. "You know about this?"

She shook her head, vehemently. "Not a thing. I think I recognize some of those people down there, though."

158

I squinted, and sure enough, I thought I saw Max. And, next to him . . . was that *Blue?*

Suddenly, a chubby, middle-aged man with a gray pony-tail tried to break away from the crowd and run up the hill toward us. Max stuck out a foot as he passed, and the guy hit the ground, and then rolled backwards. The crowd cleared a path for him, and he ended up in a pile of brush underneath the sign.

I looked at Grandma. "I think they're waiting for us. You wanna go down?"

"I'm not sure," she said, shading her eyes. "I think I see Frank down there. I bet he's pissed about the car. And the weed."

"Come on," I said, curiosity taking top position in my brain. "It's not like we hurt it or anything. And he did give it to you to take care of. It needs to be taken out for a spin once in a while, just to keep it in good shape. You took all your spins at once."

Pixie danced up to the car just then, and gave us a merry grin. "Come on, come on. Get out of the frickin' car already." She waved her arms like she was ushering us into a fancy restaurant, and I opened the door and stepped out. Music broke out wildly – and badly. Was that a fucking marching band down there? It was, and it was playing *Don't Want to Miss a Thing* at the top of its out-of-tune collective minds.

I turned to Pixie, who was enjoying the hell out of the whole spectacle. "What do you know about this?"

She smiled. "A couple of your friends wanted to meet you here and surprise you. That's all I know."

By now, we were halfway down the slope, and the crowd was

159

drawing closer as well. It reminded me of my recent acid trip, when I was dressed in robes like a female Moses, and the world was spread at my feet.

The marching band was straggling desperately after the rest of the crowd, throwing off occasional blinding flashes as sunlight struck their instruments. It was like slogging through quicksand to reach Max and Blue, who led the pack, but we finally got there.

"You made it, Mobile One!" exclaimed Max, wrapping his arms around Grandma Rose and me.

Blue just looked at me. "Babe."

And I did something I would have bet you cash money just a week ago that I would never do again. I threw my arms – and legs – around him, and kissed him like I was starving to death for want of his mouth on mine.

When I finally pulled my mouth away from his, I looked him in the eye. "I want back in."

He grinned. "You were never out, babe."

The pudgy bastard had finally reached us, and he thrust a wireless mic in my face. "Eve Petra! I'm the general Manager of KLSK, LA's premier classic rock station. I'd like to offer you a morning show--"

He was interrupted by a much skinnier guy, also with a silver ponytail. "Forget him! I can give you a column that will go out to every alternative paper in the country. No censorship, complete control over content, and a percentage of the syndication deal. What do you say?"

From behind him, Peter Beater, of all people, stepped forward. He cleared his throat and looked embarrassed. "Eve, I made a terrible mistake in letting you go. You're what everyone loves about *Whipt!*, and I want you back. Double your salary, and write whatever you want. You can even set

Loyola's desk on fire again." He held out a hand to shake in one of those, 'all is forgiven' gestures.

I climbed off of Blue and looked my suitors over.

"Why are you two guys so interested in me, all of a sudden? As a matter of fact, why do you even know who I am? I've never met either of you." I turned to Beater. "And what on earth made you change your mind, fuckhead?" Beater didn't even turn red. He just kept giving me a jittery smile.

All of a sudden, everyone was looking at Max and Blue.

I tapped my foot. "Okay, out with it. What you have guys been up to?"

Max looked uncomfortable. "Well, you were emailing me about your trip every night, and Blue started dropping by, trying to figure out how to get a hold of you. He missed you, and you weren't calling him back. . ."

"So he let me read your emails," continued Blue.

I was still tapping, and still clueless. "And how does *that* explain all of *this?*" I asked, indicating the gathered crowd with my hand. Another cheer went up, this one a little more ragged. We were loosing 'em on the curve. Somebody in the marching band crashed a cymbal.

Blue looked me in the eye. "You know I told you I was thinking about picking up a syndication service? I did. And I ran your emails as a column."

Max was blushing. "I, ah, told him you said it was okay."

I turned back to Blue. "And?"

"And it turned into a nationwide craze! Overnight, everybody in the country couldn't wait to see what happened to you next. And everyone you wrote about turned into instant celebrities. Even Duran Duran's record sales shot up. The Hairy Bear Hotel is booked up for the next two years. Lick's

161

House has people sleeping in the attic, just to get in. And Antler's Wild Men seminars have already had to franchise to handle the traffic. The pocket protector guy – Dicker? His stock has split twice."

My head was swimming as I tried to sort it out. "Okay, let me get this straight. I get fired, leave Detroit in a haze of shame and disgrace, unable to get a job anywhere, and you start sharing my most personal, private emails with a guy I swore ten years ago I was never goin' to let into my head again?"

Max grinned and nodded. "Yep, you got that part."

I turned to Blue. "And you, fully aware of how fucked up I was, took those personal, private emails, and plastered them all over the *country?*"

Blue nodded too, although he was a little more cautious in the grinning department.

"And now I'm a huge success all across America, and everybody and their mother is begging me to come work for them, including the scum-bag ex-boss who fired me in the first place?"

Now they were both nodding in unison.

I looked at Peter the Beater. "Get down on your knees and beg."

Without a second's hesitation, he did. "Please, Eve, I need you back. I'll pay you anything you want."

I grabbed the mic in the KLSK guy's hand. "Say that again."

He did, right into the mic.

I pulled the microphone away and put it to my own mouth. "Fuck. In. No."

The crowd cheered wildly, and I jacked my arms triumphantly in the air. "I've had a lot of time to think on this trip. And I've learned a lot. I learned that the world has been changing all around me, and I've been too busy

162

hiding in a Jack Daniels' bottle to see it. Did you guys all know there's no music on MTV anymore?"

There was a chorus of lusty boos.

"I didn't. I didn't know that I didn't have to crystallize my whole life around something bad that happened to me when I was just four. I didn't know I was free to do anything that I wanted. To fall in love, and stay in love." I glanced at Blue, who had that same look on his face that he had the first time we made love. "I didn't know that I could let my heart rip open, and live through it. That's happening right now. Guess what? I'm still alive."

I paced for a minute, gathering my thoughts. "And you know what else I found out? I found out I don't need to be a black leather poser, or write a column and have an image, in order to have a life. Which is exactly what I plan on doing, as of now!"

There was more cheering, and the band broke into *Amazing*, which made my ears cry, but hey. I looked at Blue. "How sold are you on this whole syndication thing?"

He shrugged. "Freddie's looking after it for me at the moment. He's kind of got a talent. What do you have in mind?"

Before I could answer him, a youngish guy – maybe late twenties – stepped up and shook his finger in Grandma Rose's face. "Rose, you took my car," he said, aggrieved. "You took my car, and you took my stash. Now, how you gonna explain that to me?"

"Frank," she started. "I've been storing it for you for a year. You owe me, so don't start."

"Wait a minute," I said, stepping between them. "This is Frank? What the hell is he doing at a senior center? He's a kid."

163

They both looked at me, surprised. "I never said he hung out there, Eve," explained Rosie-O. "He works there."

"For me," said a silver haired man in a nice suit and a short haircut. He was the first guy I'd seen since we stopped that was over fifty and didn't have a ponytail.

Frank blushed. "This is my dad, Frank Sr."

Frank Senior smiled at Grandma, who smiled back and batted her eyes. "I must say, young lady, I've been following your adventures just like the rest of the country, but your granddaughter never mentioned how lovely you were."

I glanced at Blue. "I was thinking about another cross country. I could keep writing it up. It's been a hell of a good time, Blue, even when I didn't know it was."

He kissed me again, which was enough of an answer for me. Then he pulled back and looked at me, puzzled. "You don't taste like Jack. What happened?"

I shrugged. "I dunno. It's hard to drive and stay smashed all the time. Parking's a bitch, for sure. I hadn't really thought about it, though."

"Did you know Aerosmith is all straight?"

"I'd heard about that, but I wasn't sure if it was true or not. They don't rock like straight guys. So, you wanna go with me?"

He kissed me again.

Grandma Rose tugged on my sleeve. "Hey, Evie, if you don't mind, Frank Senior and I are gonna drive the Roadster back to Detroit."

"Cool with me," I said. "You?"

Blue nodded. "I'm thinking RV. You, babe?"

"If the RV's rockin' don't come knockin'?"

"Exactly. But we've got one minor delay before we can get out of town."

"What do we have to do?"

"Concert. Your buddy Tyler and the rest of the guys agreed to do a private show, on one condition."

"What's the condition?"

"He wants you to explain the meaning of life to him."

*

And there you go. After we got all the detail sorted out, we spent the rest of the day hanging out with all the folks who'd been waiting to welcome us to LA. We partied under the billboard until it was time to go to the show, and took everybody with us. Even Peter the Beater loosened up and took off his tie, and I was surprised to realize I didn't bear him a grudge of any kind. After all, no harm no foul, right? And if he hadn't been such an asshole, I wouldn't have been resurrected from the rock zombie state I had been embedded in for the last two decades.

I look at it like this: I'm the original girl whose life was saved by rock-n-roll. What I thought was the destination turned out to be the launching pad, but if it hadn't been for the music, I don't think I would have made it to where I am right now.

Grandma Rose ended up marrying Frank Senior, who gave her the Roadster as a wedding gift. It was actually his, not Frank Junior's. Grandma Rose still smokes a little weed, but usually chooses champagne with her new husband instead, except when Frank Junior stops by.

Max has started painting again for real, and Vermilion Gallery is

165

now the showcase for his own work, as well as that of a few select others. Barrio continues to run drink-and-draw night, and has taken up sculpture, himself.

Freddy took over Blue's syndication business, which is doing well enough to keep us in RVs and the occasional room service, and Blue and I travel the country, doing a kind of rock and roll version of Charles Kerault's *On the Road.*

I still thank Tagaloa and Pachamana once in a while, for the brand new life. If I hadn't lived it myself, I wouldn't have believed it. Sometimes I wonder if they know each other, and this was some kind of celestial conspiracy to get me out of my rut.

I sat down the other day and figured I hadn't had a drink or so much as touched a drug in nearly a year. Damn! How the hell did that happen? But it feels good, so I keep wearing it. I was even contemplating checking out one of those AA things someday, just to see how *those* guys do it.

And I still keep in touch with Steven, who's turned out to be a hell of a nice guy, although he doesn't always know as much as he thinks he does.

Does anybody?

The End

A HISTORY OF SARCASM

by Frank Burton

"Sometimes stories that I've used to mythologize my childhood resurface in my mind as actual memories . . . Perhaps if you tell a story enough times, it will become the truth."

This admission by Mark Greensleeves, the compulsive liar in the story, "Some Facts About Me", sums up Frank Burton's sharp, surreal and subversive short story collection, *A History of Sarcasm*. The seventeen stories in this collection blur the boundaries between fact and fantasy through a series of obsessive characters and their skewed versions of reality. Among them are a man who insists on living every aspect of his life in alphabetical order, a girl who believes she is receiving secret messages through the TV, a paranoiac who is pursued by an army of giant lobsters, and an academic who turns into a cat.

Funny, dark and relentlessly off the wall, this collection brings together the best of Frank Burton's published work with some brand new stories.

THE WOLF STEPPED OUT

By Dave Migman

Jason Irvine thinks he sees things as they really are. He sees the goddess of decay clasping the city's industrial zones and he deciphers her messages in its cracks. The high street is his hell – but hell is always unavoidable for those who wish to understand pain.

Jason shares his flat with three no-hopers, all of them defeated and broken by the city. In his room Jason is safe. There he remembers Rosa, a Spanish girl with whom he had a brief affair while living in the countryside. She left for the city and he followed, only to be caught in the snarls of urban decay, interpreting the signs etched into the concrete.

167

But Jason's had enough. He's decided he will escape. He will find his Rosa and with her, his salvation. But the path of obsession is never clear cut. There's his tangled affair with one of his flatmates' girlfriends. There's the paranoia he encounters after being accosted by a gang of neds. Seething and stunned, he seeks sanctuary in a museum staring at a coat of banded mail. The numbers coincide, events fall into place and after a series of revelations, Jason begins work on his revenge: "the coat". His shining path to salvation.

POLLUTO

Edited by Adam Lowe

Polluto is Dog Horn Publishing's flagship literary magazine. Every quarter, editor Adam Lowe pulls together the best in anti-genre, anti-sentiment, anti-establishment lit with a wry smile and a black sense of humour.

Polluto attempts to pick apart contemporary culture via satire, subversion and passion. Each issue costs £7.99 or $11.99, and includes more fiction, poetry and colour artwork than you can shake George W. Bush at.

Past contributors have included Jeff VanderMeer, Vince Locke, Jim Steel, Allen Ashley, Andrew Hook, Rhys Hughes, Steve Redwood, Dave Migman and Deb Hoag.

If you liked *Crashin' the Real*, you'll love this!

Available direct from polluto.com.

ABOUT US

Dog Horn Publishing started from humble beginnings. Editor Ellis France (a pseudonym) decided she was bored with working in the creative industries and, well, not really creating a great deal. She was bored of stuffy offices and PR gimmicks and all that corporate bullshit.

So she set up Dog Horn Publishing in 2004, and with a team of friends and volunteers helped establish cult author R. L. Royle with her first two publica-

168

tions: *Lucy's Monster* and *Eleven Terrible Months*. Both of these early titles were limited editions, both of which are now pretty valuable.

In 2007, Ellis decided to step down to pursue pastures new, and journalist, writer and editor Adam Lowe stepped up to the plate. Continuing the limited edition design ethic, he released the lushly-produced and ultra-exclusive *Polluto*, which was released in January 2008 with contributors such as Jeff VanderMeer and Vince Locke.

Since then, Adam decided to expand the booklist, and subsequent publications were released in trade paperback format worldwide. *Crashin' the Real* is the first of these trade editions, and we hope you've enjoyed reading it as much as we did when it first slithered through the aether into our hands.

Long live the Dog!

Visit us online at doghorn.com.

169

BITE LIKE A BITCH!
Join the Book Club Now!

If you liked this book, have you considered taking out a subscription to the Dog Horn Book Club? For your subscription you'll get the next six Dog Horn titles as soon as they're published and receive regular updates about our authors and products.

To join the Dog Horn Book Club, send a cheque for £50.00 (£55.00 in Europe and £60.00 in the USA/rest of world) to Dog Horn Publishing, 45 Monk Ings, Birstall, Batley, WF17 9HU, United Kingdom. Make cheques payable to Dog Horn Publishing. Alternatively, send payment via PayPal to editor@doghornpublishing.com.

To order single titles, cut out or photocopy the order form below and post to us:

Please send me the following Dog Horn Publishing titles:

A History of Sarcasm by Frank Burton -   Paperback (£9.99) __
Mister Gum by Rhys Hughes -   Paperback (£9.99) __
The Wolf Stepped Out by Dave Migman -   Paperback (£9.99) __
Hemorrhaging Slave of an Obese Eunuch by Tom Bradley -
                                                  Paperback (£9.99) __
The Bride Stripped Bare by Rachel Kendall -
                                                  Paperback (£9.99) __
Broken Symmetries by Steve Redwood -   Paperback (£12.99) __

Please include P&P of £2.00 + £1.50 for each additional title. For European addresses, include £2.50 + £1.75 for each additional title, and for the US and rest of world, include £3.00 + £2.00 for each additional title.

Shipping Total: ____
Grand Total: _____

ND - #0503 - 270225 - C0 - 234/156/14 - PB - 9781907133008 - Matt Lamination